Mail Order M[...]

Book 43 in Brides of [...]

Kirsten Osbourne

Copyright © 2023 by Kirsten Osbourne

Unlimited Dreams Publishing

All rights reserved.

Cover design by Erin Dameron Hill/ EDH Graphics

No part of this book may be reproduced in any form or by any electronic or mechanical means including information storage and retrieval systems, without permission in writing from the author. The only exception is by a reviewer, who may quote short excerpts in a review.

This book is a work of fiction. Names, characters, places, and incidents either are products of the author's imagination or are used fictitiously. Any resemblance to actual persons, living or dead, events, or locales is entirely coincidental.

Kirsten Osbourne

Visit my website at www.kirstenandmorganna.com

Printed in the United States of America

Sign up for instant notification of all of Kirsten's New Releases Text 'BOB' to 42828

And

For a complete list of Kirsten's works head to her website wwww.kirstenandmorganna.com

Chapter One

Betsy O'Brien stepped out of the church and watched longingly as her sister Darla drove off with her new husband, the buggy they drove in dragging tin cans behind them.

Betsy had been in love with Benjamin, Darla's new husband, for as long as she could remember. For a while, she'd been sure he felt the same about her, but he'd been interested in her sister all along.

Darla had a sparkling personality and boys always surrounded her at dances, at recess from school...everywhere she went boys surrounded her. It was enough to make Betsy spit, but she wouldn't because she was too much of a lady for that.

All four of Betsy's sisters looked a great deal like Betsy, with the same brown hair, but they all had special things that made them stand out. Her oldest sister, Ruth, was brilliant. Easily the smartest girl in school, she'd gone on to college, where she'd fallen in love with a boy from the men's university in town and married him.

Then there was Darla, who had a personality no one could overlook. Betsy was right smack in the middle of the O'Brien sisters, and there was nothing remarkable about her.

Then came Sally, who was a tomboy in every sense of the word. She was engaged to a man she'd met while fishing one afternoon. He said he was very impressed by any lady who could put her own worm on a fish hook. Of course, Sally had only agreed to marry him when he'd promised her he would allow her to wear bloomers in public. Mother would never let any of her little ladies run around in bloomers.

Last but not least was Shirly. Shirly had been an artist from the first time she'd picked up a pencil. She was known throughout Massachusetts for her paintings. An art collector from Boston had seen one of her paintings on display, and the two had struck up a correspondence, and finally had married.

Only one O'Brien sister was left. Betsy. She was the quiet one, who read books in her spare time. The one who didn't have an escort for every dance. The one people overlooked.

She stifled tears as her last sister left for her honeymoon. Her mother was beside her and completely oblivious to her pain. "Let's go home, Betsy. Goodness knows you'll be the daughter who will stay at home forever."

Betsy heard the words and could think of nothing more horrible than that fate. She wanted to be able to live her own life. Not live with her parents for the rest of her days.

As she followed her mother, she noticed Elizabeth and Bernard Tandy there, off to one side. They'd been invited to attend the wedding not so much because they were friends but because they were affluent.

On a whim, she said, "You go on, Mother. I see a friend I haven't spoken with in a while. I'll catch up."

"Whatever you want, dear. Don't stay out too late." Mother rarely cared what Betsy did. Why it seemed as if she'd given up on her middle daughter.

Betsy moved across the street to talk to Mrs. Tandy. "Hello," she said tentatively. "I know we've never actually spoken but I'm..."

"Betsy O'Brien!" Mrs. Tandy exclaimed. "Are you doing all right?"

Betsy was taken aback by the question. "Yes, of course. Why do you ask?"

"Well, given that your sister just married the man you thought was the love of your life, it would make perfect sense if you were not all right." Mrs. Tandy handed the baby in her arms to her husband. "Let's walk and talk, Betsy."

"I...how do you know?"

"I'm a very observant person. It helps in my line of work. You know what I do, don't you?"

Betsy blushed and nodded. "It's why I wanted to talk to you."

"I had a feeling that was the case. Are you thinking about becoming a mail-order bride?" Mrs. Tandy asked sweetly.

After a moment, Betsy gave a firm nod. "I feel as if I've spent my entire life living in the shadow of my sisters. Now that they're gone, my sunburn is going to be atrocious."

Mrs. Tandy laughed. "You're very funny. All right. Do you mind if the man you go to has been married before? Maybe a couple of children are involved?"

"Oh, I would adore that immensely. I've always been extremely fond of children. I just... well, I've always been too shy to approach a man, and my sisters always caught the attention of all the men...which left me alone."

"And I'm sure you've no desire to live with your mother forever," Elizabeth said. "I do understand that. If you remember, I'm the second eldest of the Miller children. You know..."

"The demon horde? Oh, yes, everyone remembers that."

"Well, then you know I understand the need to stand on my own two feet and not spend your life living with your parents."

"Do you have someone you think would suit me?"

"I do, actually. If you have time, come home with me, and I'll show you the letter. Mr. Marvin Small if I remember correctly, and I usually do."

The Tandys only lived one street over from Betsy and her parents. "Yes, of course." Her mother wouldn't mind if she was out late. She probably wouldn't even notice.

When they reached the largest house in all of Beckham, Massachusetts, Mrs. Tandy strode straight down the hall to the last door on the left. "This is my office, and it's where I keep all my correspondence. Please, have a seat."

"I do hope you have someone in mind who will not care that I'm very shy."

Mrs. Tandy nodded. "I do." She found the letter she was looking for and handed it to Betsy. "Read this and tell me what you think."

Betsy took the letter and read over it quickly.

Dear Potential Bride,

My name is Marvin Small, and I'm a widower with two children, Cassandra and Tommy, aged thirteen and nine respectively. Cassandra is a sad, shy, withdrawn girl. More than I need a wife, she needs a mother. Someone who will answer her questions and love her as her own. My wife died three years ago, and my mother has been living with us since then, but my mother has gone back east to her own life, not enjoying the quiet nights here in Wyoming.

I'm a rancher, so there was no way I could follow her, and I wasn't going to allow my only daughter to be that far from me. I'm a decent looking fellow with a full head of hair and all my own teeth.

If you think you could mother two children you didn't give birth to and be a good wife to a desperate man, I'd love to have you. Please have the matchmaker wire me when you want to come, and I'll make certain she gets paid, and you have funds to get here.

I hope you'll reply quickly because I truly need your help.

Sincerely,

Marvin Small

Betsy read the letter once more, a small smile transforming her face into one of beauty. Finally, she nodded. "I'd like to marry him."

"I thought you would. Would you like me to wire him?" Mrs. Tandy asked.

"Yes, please."

"Will your parents mind if you do this without their permission?"

Betsy took a deep breath. "Mrs. Tandy, I'm twenty-two years old. I've never had a beau. My mother has given up on me finding a man, and has started to talk to me about growing old with her."

"Call me Elizabeth." She reached out and covered Betsy's hand with hers. "You are a beautiful woman, and any man would be thrilled to have you. It doesn't matter that you're twenty-two or that you've never had a beau. When you go west, you will find that you will be a wonderful mother to Marvin's daughter. It's a big step, but I believe it's just what you need to come out of your shell."

Betsy smiled and nodded. "I do believe you're right."

"I will go and wire him now, and see if we can get you on a train out within the week. Or would you like more time?"

"Monday would suit me well. Two days is enough time to get all my belongings packed and be on my way."

"I will make the arrangements. I'll send my husband with a note when we know exactly when you're leaving. Will that work for you?"

Betsy felt like the weight of the world was suddenly off her shoulders. She could travel far away and be with people who had never met her. Or more importantly, who had never met her sisters. For once, she could just be Betsy and not one of the O'Brien girls. Or someone's sister. It would be glorious!

On her walk home, Betsy daydreamed about what it would be like to be so far away from home. She could be her own self and no one would compare her even one iota. Life was going to be wonderful. She could feel it deep down in her bones.

When she arrived home, she went into the parlor where her mother was working on some needlework. It was pretty much all her mother did except tell the cooks and maids what to do.

"Mother, I need to talk to you about something."

"All right," Mother said without even looking up from her embroidery.

"I've decided to move west and get married."

"That's nice, dear."

"I'm going to start packing today, and I'll leave on Monday." Betsy hated when her mother didn't pay attention to her when she spoke.

"Leave for where?" Mother finally looked up and saw that Betsy was serious. "You don't have anywhere to go."

"I just told you. I'm going to Wyoming, and I'm getting married."

Mother looked perplexed. "But you don't know anyone in Wyoming. Where could you possibly have met?"

"I spoke with Mrs. Tandy after the wedding. She's arranging for me to go west to marry a man named Marvin Small." Betsy felt satisfied by the look of shock on her mother's face. It was about time someone paid attention to her.

"But...you can't be a mail-order bride. Our family is wealthy. That's for women who have nothing else in their lives. You have us."

"Do I really?" Betsy asked.

"Whatever is that supposed to mean?"

Betsy sighed. "Nothing. I'm going to my room to pack now."

"I have not given you permission to go!"

"I'm not asking for it, Mother. I'm twenty-two years old, and this is almost the nineteenth century. If I want to marry, I need not ask your permission." With that, Betsy went to her room and pulled out the trunk she'd gotten when her mother had sent her away to finishing school. She'd felt finished both before and after school. What it was supposed to have done for her was still a mystery.

She was half-finished packing the trunk before she realized her mother hadn't bothered to follow her. It was for the best though. She was not going to change her mind.

It was less than an hour later when there was a knock on her door. One of the maids handed her a folded sheet of paper. "I'm to tell you it's from Mrs. Tandy."

"Thank you, Greta." Greta had always been her favorite of the maids. She treated Betsy as if she was a person in her own right and not just part of the five-headed beast that was the O'Brien sisters.

Sitting on her bed, she opened the note and read.

Betsy,

Mr. Small would like for you to leave Monday morning. I've taken the liberty of purchasing your fare. You will depart at ten in the morning. Bernard and I will come and collect you and your things at nine. I look forward to seeing you.

Elizabeth

Betsy hugged the note to her chest. It was really happening. She was going west, and marrying a stranger, and becoming a mother to his children. No one who knew her would understand her excitement, but it was there, and she could feel it in every inch of her body.

When everything was packed, it felt as though there had never really been anything there. All of her memories were gone, and they would leave with her. All traces of her existence were in the trunk at her feet.

She took a bath and readied herself for bed, thinking all the while about how good it would be to no longer be in Beckham, Massachusetts, a place where she'd never quite fit in. Never quite been good enough.

A whole new world was opening up for her, and she was counting down the hours until she could leave. She wasn't even surprised her father hadn't spoken to her about leaving. He didn't care more than her mother did.

Oh, they cared about all their girls in their own way. The ones they could be proud of were their favorites. So all but her and her tomboy sister Sally.

She read for a while before going to sleep. *Little Women* had been a favorite of hers for a good long while, and she was rereading it for what seemed like the thirtieth time. She understood Meg best of all. She certainly wasn't a peacemaker like Beth. Amy was more like her sister, Shirly. Jo was like Sally.

Betsy was the nondescript one who no one noticed. That was more like Meg than anyone. And she wanted to be a mother. There were no more aspirations in her world.

She had to wonder who Cassandra would be like. It would be good to get to know her. Maybe she would share her love of *Little Women*. She was a great deal more excited to be a mother than a wife. She wished the train didn't take so terribly long to get across the country. No matter though. She wasn't running from something. She was running to something.

Betsy O'Brien, the most boring of all the O'Brien sisters was running to a family and a fresh start. Soon, she would be there. There would be no more nights all alone with no one to talk to. No more days of sitting and sewing with her mother, with neither of them having anything to say to the other.

She took the tablet she kept on a table beside her bed, and wrote how she felt at that moment.

> *For the first time in my memory, I'm full of hope. Hope for my future. For so long, I've lived in the shadow of my sisters, and though I love them all dearly, I need the opportunity to be my own person. No more will I be called that other O'Brien girl because people can't remember my name.*
>
> *No, I will simply be Betsy Small. Wife and mother. My joy knows no bounds.*

Chapter Two

The train ride to Wyoming seemed as if it took months. Betsy was thrilled to see the country, though, and she kept busy by making herself a couple of aprons, which she knew she'd need once she reached her destination.

She was traveling to Cody, Wyoming, where Marvin was to meet the train and drive her home to his ranch an hour out of Cody. At least that's what Elizabeth had told her as they drove to the train station.

She was startled when the conductor called out Cody, Wyoming. She hadn't expected to be so close, but she wasn't about to complain about it. Walking to the front of the train, her legs felt as if they were going to give out. She should have accepted her father's offer of a sleeping car, but she had a feeling she'd be living with no wealth, so there was no reason for her to wait to get used to her new way of life.

She accepted the conductor's hand to help her down off the train, her eyes scanning the crowd for someone looking for a stranger.

Finally, she spotted a boy and a girl with a wooden sign held between them that read, "Betsy O'Brien." She smiled and walked toward them, noting that the girl seemed very withdrawn, as if she'd rather be anywhere else in the world, while the boy seemed excited to meet her. She couldn't see a man near them, so she spoke to the two children. "I'm Betsy O'Brien."

"Nice to meet you, Miss O'Brien," the boy, Tommy, said.

"It's nice to meet you as well, Tommy." Betsy looked expectantly at Cassandra, who was looking at the ground. "Do you prefer to be called Candy or Cassandra?"

"Everyone calls her Candy, but she don't talk much," Tommy told her.

"Is your pa near?" Betsy asked, hoping he hadn't sent his children to fetch her instead of coming himself.

A man approached carrying what looked like her trunk. She smiled at him, a full smile, not the kind of shy smile she was used to sharing with a man. She'd practiced it on the train. "Mr. Small?" she asked, realizing his name didn't suit him at all. Why, he must be well over six feet tall.

"Miss O'Brien. I see you've met the children. The pastor here in town is waiting to perform our marriage ceremony. I hope that meets your needs."

"Yes, of course," Betsy said. "Thank you for retrieving my trunk for me."

"My pleasure. Let me put this in the wagon, and then we'll drive to the church. It's only about a mile, and I'd walk it if we didn't have all of your earthly belongings in the back of the wagon."

"I'll stay with it, Pa. I don't mind," Tommy offered.

"You'll come to the wedding with the rest of us," Marvin said, shaking his head. "You know I want you there."

Tommy sighed and acted very put out by the answer. "I know."

Cassandra still hadn't said a word, and Betsy could see she had her work cut out for her. It wouldn't be easy to get this child to talk to her, and would be even harder to become her friend. She was determined to make it happen though.

Once in the wagon, Marvin drove them through Cody, having to stop the wagon for men fighting in the streets more than once. Suddenly, Betsy was glad she wasn't going to have to spend much time in the rough western town.

As soon as the wagon stopped, the children got down out of the back, but Betsy waited for Marvin to come around and offer his hand. She gripped it and he helped her to the ground. "I think you'll like Pastor Hoffman. He's not our regular pastor as we go to a small church in the country just a mile or two down the road from the ranch, but he's a nice enough man, and he was willing to perform the ceremony."

"I'm sure I'll like him just fine," Betsy said, her eye catching Candy, who was looking only at the ground.

Walking into the church, Marvin called out, "Pastor! We're here for our wedding."

"Come on then!" The pastor called back.

The pastor was an older gentleman with gray hair and merry blue eyes. They seemed to dance as he spoke, which was very welcoming in Betsy's opinion.

"You must be Betsy," the pastor said.

"Yes, I'm Betsy O'Brien."

"It's very good to meet you, Betsy. Are you ready to get married?"

Betsy nodded. "I'm ready for the whole journey to be over. It takes a very long time to get from Massachusetts to Cody, Wyoming."

"I'm sure it does. Well, I'm glad you're here. And I'm sure this family is as well." The pastor looked at Marvin. "Let's do this."

Candy thrust a bouquet of flowers into Betsy's hand, and Betsy smiled at the girl who stood beside her. "Thank you so much."

Candy didn't respond. Instead, she looked at the floor, not even willing to make eye contact.

The ceremony was quick and painless. Betsy was surprised that in her vows the pastor asked her to promise to love the children as well as Marvin. That was the easiest promise she'd ever had to make. Already her heart was breaking for Candy.

When the pastor told Marvin, he could kiss the bride, Marvin smiled down into her face, lifted her chin up, and he kissed her. It wasn't a passionate kiss like she'd heard her sisters talking about, but was more of a soft kiss. Betsy was glad, because it was her first, and she had no idea what she would have done if the kiss had been passionate in the middle of a church. It would have struck her as very strange, especially with the children watching.

They headed back out to the wagon, and Marvin helped Betsy inside. "Well, that seemed painless," she said.

Marvin chuckled. "Most weddings are painful?"

"The last one I attended was," Betsy said honestly, offering no more details than that. Marvin seemed to accept her answer for what it was.

"I can't wait to get you home and show you around. The children attend school in the church near us. If the weather is at all bad, they are not to go. There are too many storms that blow up out of nowhere, and I'm not risking my children."

"Of course not. There's nothing more precious than your children."

"Our children," he said. "I really would like for you to think of them that way. Most decisions about them will be made by you. You will be their primary caretaker. I run a large ranch, and have thirty men working for me. I don't have time to be bothered with small decisions."

"All right. I'll happily take on their care."

The entire way home, he talked about the children, explaining that Cassandra had been afraid of her own shadow since the day her mother had died. "You'll need to help her gain her confidence. Mother tried, but she was unable to make Candy any more confident. Candy knew she was always going to leave, and I don't think Candy could fully trust mother as a result."

"I understand. I will do my very best with her." Betsy hadn't realized quite how bad it was, but she was more than willing to help Candy come out of her shell and be less afraid.

"Tommy seems to be handling things fine. He was much younger when Lynn died though." He shook his head. "I would love to take some of Tommy's lack of fear and instill it into Candy, but that's not possible."

"Of course. I'm not a miracle worker, but I do adore children, and I'll be happy to do all I can for both of them."

"Good. Kristen will be there to take care of the house and cook all the meals. Really, your only responsibility will be the children. School starts in another month, and Candy gets very agitated before school starts. And during school."

"I won't be cooking and cleaning?" Betsy asked. She'd had no idea he had someone who did the housework.

"No, you won't. Kristen handles all that. Does that bother you?" Marvin asked.

"No, of course not. I grew up with servants, but I didn't expect to have them here. I think it'll be good for me though."

"I would like you to sew for the children, if you don't mind. Try and teach Candy what she needs to know to be a wife."

"She doesn't have a boy in mind, does she?"

He laughed. "No. At her age, if she did, I'd have to throttle the boy."

Betsy smiled at that. Her father had been the same when she and her sisters were small. "I don't blame you."

"Tell me a little about you. Were you an only child?" he asked.

"No, I was the third of five daughters. I grew up in Beckham, Massachusetts, and my family and I spent every summer living in a house on the ocean. Father would come and join us on the weekends, but he'd travel back to town every Monday."

"What does your father do?"

"He's a businessman. He owns a few stores in Beckham and some in Boston as well."

"Well, that's interesting. Did you ever help him with his business?" Marvin asked.

"I wish he'd have allowed that. Instead, I spent all my time learning needlepoint. Mother sent me away to finishing school when I was sixteen because she was afraid I was too quiet to ever marry. I certainly understand how Candy feels."

"Finishing school must have helped you a great deal then. You don't seem at all shy to me."

Betsy smiled at his words. "Not particularly. I didn't like it there, and I would never recommend sending any girl there. I am working on the shyness is all I can say." And of course her sisters weren't there to make her feel inadequate. That made a big difference.

"Well, I hope you can teach my Candy to do the same. She's a smart girl, and she always had friends surrounding her. After her mother died, I think she was simply afraid that everyone else in her life would leave too, and so she's formed a little shell around herself that she prefers to never emerge from."

"My heart breaks for her. Perhaps I can help her." Betsy took a deep breath. "How does she do at school? Does she have friends now?"

"No, and she hates every minute of it. Every morning she gets up and begs me not to make her go. I wish I felt like she could stay home, but I want her to be educated." Marvin shook his head. "I just don't know what to do any longer."

"How would you feel if we gave her the option of me teaching her at home? Every school uses the same textbooks. I have mine from when I was a girl, and I was a good student." Not as good as her eldest sister, but good. Betsy was at the top of her class without scaring people with how smart she was.

"That may be a good idea. At least until she can work through some of her issues. I so worry that she'll want to spend the rest of her life locked in her room and never interacting with anyone. It would be a shame."

"I'll talk to her about me tutoring her tomorrow. If she likes the idea, she can calm down about school because I'll be there for her. When did your mother leave to go back east?"

"When school was out in June. I wanted her to stay through the summer, but she said she'd spent enough time here helping, and she needed to get back to her own life."

"Which is understandable," Betsy said. "It had to be hard for her not to be home."

"I guess."

"I know it would be hard for my mother. She has friends she has tea with on different days of the week. There are meetings she attends. I don't know what all she did."

Marvin frowned. "What about your sisters? What did they do?"

"All of my sisters are married. They spent time with their future husbands and worked on whatever project was in their mind. Then they married and moved away, and I don't know what they do all day now."

"I see. Well, I'm glad you didn't marry young so you could come and help with my family."

"Our marriage...will we share a room?" It was hard for Betsy to ask the question, but she did better when she knew what was expected of her.

"Yes, we will. I know ours is an unorthodox kind of marriage, but I still expect you to...well, some women call them wifely duties."

Betsy swallowed hard. She understood that men needed certain things from their wives, and though she had come mostly to be a mother to his children, it certainly wouldn't kill her to allow him to take care of his needs. She'd heard her sisters whispering about liking what they did with their husbands when Mother wasn't listening.

"All right."

"All right? You're not going to argue with me?" Marvin looked at her with a grin.

"No. I rarely argue. I just proceed to show people that I'm right. It's much simpler that way."

He laughed at that. "Now I understand what I'm getting into here! How did your parents feel about you coming west to marry a stranger?"

"Mother thought I'd lost my mind and told me I couldn't come, but I told her I was, and I did."

"It's nice to see a woman who knows her own mind. I think I made the right choice of brides."

"Were there other women who you were thinking of marrying?" Betsy asked.

"There were a couple of local women who set their cap for me, but they weren't the right person to help my Candy. So I made it clear I wasn't interested, and I wrote to a matchmaker."

"Who I went to and asked to find me a husband."

"Why did you do that?" he asked.

She shrugged. "I didn't have a real identity back east. My sisters were all more...well, just more than me. People would look at me and know I was the other O'Brien girl. No one remembered my name or anything about me. All of my sisters and I have the same coloring, so we were always compared to one another."

"You will definitely have your own identity here." He shook his head. "I think people thought too little of you back east. I got my first look at you and thought you were magnificent. Your beauty, the way you carry yourself. You are exactly the wife I need. My magnificent bride."

"Thank you," Betsy said softly. She certainly hoped he still felt the same way when he got to know her better.

Chapter Three

When they pulled up in front of a huge house, Betsy was stunned for a moment. She'd thought she was going from a life of affluence to a life of poverty, but it seemed she had married a man just as wealthy, if not wealthier, than her father.

Marvin helped her down from the wagon before enlisting Tommy to help him carry the trunk inside. Betsy turned to Candy. "Perhaps you could show me around?"

Candy nodded, but her eyes didn't lift from the floor. She led Betsy inside, where there was a closet and a hall. Leading Betsy down the hall, she pointed to a parlor. "What a lovely parlor."

Candy kept walking. At the end of the hall in one direction was the kitchen, and in the other direction was the dining room. The house was much more casual than her parents, and it felt like a place Betsy could call a home.

"Is there a cellar?" Betsy asked.

Candy nodded.

Betsy hoped the girl would speak to her soon, but she was starting to realize Candy was a lot worse off than she'd imagined from the letter Marvin had sent.

There was a room off of the kitchen, and Betsy walked toward it. "Which room is this?" There, a question that couldn't be answered with yes or no.

Candy didn't look at her as she mumbled her answer. "Kristen's room."

"And Kristen is the housekeeper?" Betsy confirmed, trying not to clap her hands that the girl had actually spoken to her.

Candy nodded.

"All right." It was afternoon, and the house was spotless. Perhaps Kristen took a few hours off in the middle of the day.

Candy started up the stairs and Betsy was behind her. The first door was a bedroom. When Candy opened the door, she saw it was obviously Marvin's bedroom—the bedroom she would share with her new husband. There was an empty room next, and then on the left, Candy's room and on the right, Tommy's room. At the very end of the hall was the bathroom.

"I was hoping there would be indoor plumbing here!" Betsy exclaimed.

Candy smiled slightly for the first time since they'd entered the house.

"Your pa and I talked on the way here. How would you feel about me teaching you at home this year? Or you could go to school. We're leaving the choice completely up to you."

Candy looked at her for a moment, and once she ascertained that Betsy wasn't joking, she said, "Oh, yes! Please teach me at home."

"Then that's what I'll do. Your brother will still go to school every day, and if you decide you want to do the same, that would be fine. It wouldn't hurt my feelings at all."

Candy's face looked more relaxed after that, though she still wasn't at all chatty. She answered questions directed to her and no others. When she got downstairs, she asked, "When does school start?"

She didn't see Marvin anywhere, so she turned to Tommy for her answer. "September second."

Counting the days in her head, she knew that it was August twenty third. So they had nine days or so. "That gives me two weeks to get you ready. Do you need new shoes? New clothes?"

Tommy shook his head. "No. I just got last year's clothes broken in good."

"I am going to look through your clothes and see if I agree with you."

Tommy groaned. "I should have known you'd act just like a mother." With that, he turned and headed outside.

"Be home in time for supper!" Betsy called after him.

At the mention of food, Betsy realized she hadn't eaten since supper the night before, and she was hungry. She went into the kitchen, aware that Candy was following immediately behind her. "I'm hungry," Betsy told her shadow. She looked in the ice box in the corner of the room and found a piece of cheese. There was what looked to be day old bread on the counter. "The cook we had growing up taught me to make a delicious sandwich from bread, butter, and cheese. It's a hot sandwich. Would you like to try one?"

Candy nodded.

Betsy rummaged around for a frying pan and found the butter. She put the pan on the stove and added just a little of the ball of butter, and then she buttered four slices of bread. The butter was sizzling as she cut the cheddar cheese into slices, put two slices of bread, butter down, onto the pan. She arranged the cheese on each slice, and then added another piece to the top of each sandwich with the butter side up.

"This is the yummiest sandwich in the whole world," Betsy said as she flipped the sandwiches and they sizzled against the pan.

When she took them off the stove, she put them on two small plates, and they sat down at the table right there in the kitchen to eat them. Betsy sighed as she ate her first bite. It tasted just like Jacqueline, the cook's, did.

Candy looked at the sandwich skeptically before picking it up and taking a bite. A smile crossed her face as she took another.

"Delicious, aren't they?"

Candy nodded.

"I won't always cook at odd times, but I realized I hadn't eaten since last night, and I was hungry."

As they ate, Betsy talked to the girl, trying to put her at ease. "When I was a girl, and I would get overwhelmed by my four sisters,

I would hide in the kitchen. Finally, our cook decided to teach me to cook because of the sheer amount of time I was spending in the kitchen. I'm glad I know how to make simple meals now though. If I get hungry in the middle of the night, I can sneak down to the kitchen and make myself something to eat."

Candy nodded. "You can teach me."

"Do you want to learn to cook?" Already Candy seemed a great deal more relaxed knowing she didn't have to go to school.

Candy nodded.

"What about sewing? Needlepoint? Cleaning? All the things that would make you a good wife."

Candy nodded again. "Grandmother said it was beneath me to learn all those things."

"Well, that's not true at all!" Betsy shook her head. "What if you decide to go hiking and get lost in the woods? You need to know how to both find food and cook it. How else will you survive?"

Candy grinned, shrugging.

"Well, I'll teach you anything you need to know. We'll do your schoolwork, and we'll add in anything else you want to learn. If I don't know how to do something, I'm sure Kristen will teach us both."

Candy's eyes widened, and she shook her head.

"Why not?" Betsy felt like it was the easiest solution.

"Kristen only speaks Norwegian."

Betsy blinked a few times. "How will I instruct her on what I want her to fix for supper?"

Candy shrugged. "Kristen cooks what she wants to cook. I hate lutefisk."

"Well, we'll work on teaching her some English then. How long has she worked for your family?"

"Since before Ma died."

"I know you miss your ma. And I know I would be a poor substitute for her, so I don't even want you to call me Ma. Calling me Betsy will work out so much better."

"You really don't mind?"

Betsy shook her head. "I think it's for the best. If you ever want to call me Ma, you may, but we'll start out with my given name."

"Thank you," Candy said softly.

"Oh, I think we're going to be fast friends."

"I hope so."

Kristen came out of her room then, glaring at Betsy and shaking her finger at the plates in front of them. She took the plates into the kitchen, though there were a couple of bites left on Candy's plate.

Betsy looked at Candy with wide eyes. "Is she always like that?" Betsy asked in a whisper. She didn't know why she whispered since Kristen couldn't speak English, but it felt best to whisper when talking about someone who could hear.

Candy nodded.

"Then we should go sit in the parlor, and we'll talk about what we want to do for school this year." Betsy got up and walked toward the parlor, having no doubt Candy was following along behind her.

When they reached the parlor, they took seats beside each other on the sofa. "Tell me what you'd like to learn. If I can teach it, I will."

The first thing Candy did was point to a beautiful piano in one corner of the room. "My ma was teaching me to play before she died. I loved it. Can you teach me?"

Betsy nodded. "I took piano lessons from the time I was four until last year. I love the piano."

Candy looked excited.

"What else do you want to learn?"

"Cooking, sewing, how to act like a lady when you're courted by a boy."

"Do you have a particular boy in mind?" Betsy asked.

"I do."

"Well, you need to know right now that I don't think young girls should marry. I think the youngest would be around eighteen, but I also think it's better to wait a little while."

Candy nodded. "I need to learn how to...let a boy know I'm interested."

"I think I can teach you that."

They spent the rest of the afternoon simply chatting, and though she thought about pulling out needlework to show Candy how to embroider, she decided against it. Instead, she gave Candy her full attention and the girl opened up to her. Not completely. But so much more than Betsy had expected on their first day together.

Shortly before six, Tommy came barreling into the house. "Did I miss supper?"

Betsy shook her head. "Not unless we both missed it as well."

Marvin wandered into the house a few minutes later. He didn't seem to have Tommy's need to get everywhere immediately. "I'll wash my hands and be ready for supper." He didn't ask what they were having, probably because he knew no one knew except Kristen.

When they all gathered for supper, Kristen didn't eat with the family. Betsy made it clear she was welcome, but Kristen shook her head and went back into the kitchen. Betsy looked at the food in front of her and decided not to ask what it was. Instead she was going to enjoy every bite.

After the first bite, she realized it was chicken in some sort of sauce with a baked potato. It was delicious, and she saw everyone else eating the meal happily. "Candy and I have been talking. She wants to learn at home with me as her tutor, like we talked about," Betsy said.

Marvin nodded. "I think that's a very good idea,"

"But I still have to go to school?" Tommy asked.

Marvin looked at his son. "Yes, you will go to school. You don't want to stay home with a bunch of women, do you?"

Tommy looked between his sister and his new stepmother, shaking his head. "No, I like recess too much."

Betsy laughed, and she noticed Candy's lips curving into a grin as well. "Candy wants to learn all of the wifely arts as well," Betsy said. "She'll learn to cook, sew, and play the piano, as well as clean house."

Marvin nodded. "I think that's a good idea. My mother didn't think Candy should learn those things because they were below her station, whatever that means. But if my daughter is to someday be a good wife, then she needs to know those things."

Candy nodded, her face lighting up that her father liked their plan. "Thank you, Papa."

Betsy was thrilled with how Candy seemed to already be coming out of her shell a little, and she could see Marvin felt the same. This is why he'd wanted her to come be his wife, and she was glad she'd made the right choice to come there. If every day was as good as that one had been, she would be very happy with her life in Wyoming.

Just as they were finishing up their meal, Kristen carried in a cake that had been iced with flowers all over it. "Wedding Cake," Kristen said in a heavily accented voice as she went back into the kitchen.

"It's beautiful!" Betsy exclaimed.

"I thought you might like to have something special on your wedding day," Marvin said, half a smile on his face.

"Oh, yes. It's wonderful!"

Candy looked at the cake and then looked at Betsy. "I need to learn to decorate a cake that way."

Betsy shook her head. "I have no idea how to do that. Perhaps we can get Kristen to teach us if we tell her what we need."

"Even if she does understand what we want, she'll pretend not to," Candy predicted.

"Why is she so difficult?" Betsy asked.

"My wife knew enough Norwegian that she could speak with Kristen. Since she passed, Kristen does whatever she wants, and we have no idea what to do about it." Marvin shrugged. "She cooks, cleans, and takes care of us. I count myself blessed to have her."

And with those words, Betsy knew she didn't have the authority to fire Kristen or upset her. She'd make it work.

After supper, the four of them retired into the parlor. Tommy and Marvin played a game of checkers while Betsy had Candy play a few chords and do a few warm-ups on the piano. She needed to gauge the girl's skill so she could see where to pick up her lessons.

Sitting with her on the piano bench, Betsy felt close to her new stepdaughter. If they could get closer, perhaps she would be able to get Candy to where she could talk in public and return to school. She wanted Candy to be able to live a normal life with church socials, courting, and marriage. That was her goal.

When Candy began a familiar tune, Betsy matched her by playing the same one, just two octaves lower. When they finished, both of them laughing, Betsy saw a flash of surprise on Marvin's face.

Finally, it was after nine, and Marvin stood. "I think it's time for all of us to go to bed," he said.

Tommy groaned. "It's early!"

"It's not, and you know it. Bed!" He pointed in the direction of the stairs, and Tommy went reluctantly. "You too Candy."

Candy stood up from the piano bench and nodded. "Goodnight, Pa. Goodnight, Betsy."

Betsy smiled as the girl hurried toward the stairs to do as she was told.

Marv stood beside her, dumbstruck. "How did you accomplish so much in one day?"

"I let her know that I understand her feelings and fears are real. And I told her I'd do anything to help her get past them."

"Well, it certainly worked. Thank you." He reached out and drew her to him, kissing the top of her head. "You really are exactly what this family needed, my magnificent bride."

Chapter Four

Betsy was nervous as she followed Marvin up to their bedroom. She had thought he'd give her a little time to prepare for bed, but if not, she could use the bathroom. She was so thankful she didn't have to give up the sheer luxury of indoor plumbing.

Once in their bedroom, Marvin looked at her expectantly. "Do you want to take a bath before bed?"

Betsy thought about it for a moment. "Honestly, I think I'd fall asleep in the bath. I need sleep more than anything. I slept sitting up the entire way here, and a real bed sounds absolutely divine."

He frowned for a moment. "We'll put off our wedding night then. I hadn't even considered how tired you must be. I'm sorry."

She shook her head. "No, it's fine. It just hit me in the last hour or so. I'm glad I got a good start with Candy."

"Truly, that was your top priority. Go and wash up for bed. And you should take a bath in the morning."

Betsy immediately wondered if she smelled bad, but she didn't ask. She didn't want to know if the answer was yes. "I'll do that. A bath sounds wonderful, but sleep sounds even better."

She knelt on the floor in front of her trunk and pulled her nightgown from it before walking down the hall to the bathroom. The tub looked bigger than any she'd ever seen, and she longed to take the time for a nice long soak, but she really didn't think she could stay awake. She'd take her bath in the morning.

Betsy did a quick sponge bath before pulling her nightgown over her head and buttoning the top three buttons. Usually she only buttoned the top two, but she wasn't usually sleeping with a man she barely knew.

She crept back down the hall, saying a silent prayer that Marvin would either be in bed with the lights off, or he would have gone off to give her privacy. Instead, he was sitting up in bed, the covers going to his waist, and he was watching her.

She turned down the lamp on her way to the bed and climbed in beside him. It felt very strange to climb into a bed another was already in. She had never slept with another person, and she was unsure of the protocol.

"I've never slept with anyone before. Let me know if I do something I shouldn't."

Marvin looked over at his wife, barely visible by the light of the moon. "You're sharing a bed with your husband. You may do anything you wish."

"I could take your pillows?" Betsy didn't know where she found the courage, but she pulled the pillow out from behind his head and put it with her own, sighing happily. "Ahh. This is perfect."

Marvin stared down at her in disbelief for a moment before he began to laugh. "I really think I'm going to like you."

"Good, because even if you don't, you're stuck with me. We exchanged vows and promised to stay together until death do us part." She was trying not to laugh as she teased him. Who would have thought she could tease?

"Well, since you've stolen my pillow, you'll have to share with me." He moved down in the bed beside her, his head landing right next to hers on the pillow. He was facing her, and she was facing him. How strange it felt to be so close to a man.

"I don't think I said I'd share my pillows," she said, unable to keep the grin from her face.

He leaned toward her and kissed her softly. "I think I like sharing a pillow with you."

She hid a yawn behind her hand, not wanting to yawn in his face. "Just get ready for some serious snoring then…"

He chuckled. "Now, I know I like you. We're keeping you and that's all there is to it."

She giggled. "You have no choice. But you may keep me because I think I like it here."

He kissed her once more, this time his mouth opened against hers, and he touched the tip of his tongue to her lip. "I look forward to tomorrow night," he said, stroking her hair away from her face. He was glad she didn't wear it in a braid for bed. He certainly understood why women did, but he didn't have to like it. "Goodnight, Betsy."

"Goodnight, Marvin." She closed her eyes, expecting him to move back to his side of the bed, but instead, he put his arm around her and kept his head right where it was. She felt very loved, something she couldn't say she'd ever felt before.

BETSY WOKE BEFORE DAWN the following morning, as was her habit. When she opened her eyes, she realized that Marvin's head was still on the pillows they'd shared. She couldn't believe he hadn't just taken his pillow back, but instead, he'd slept close to her, and she'd loved it.

She eased herself out of bed, realizing that the house was quiet. Slipping down the hall to the bathroom, she started her bath, planning to take a quick one, as she knew the rest of the family would be waking shortly and need to use the facilities.

She washed her hair and every inch of her body, thrilled to have the opportunity to do so. There had been places to pay for a bath along the way, but she hadn't had the courage to try one. She had no idea what kind of establishments they were after all.

After her bath, she brushed her hair and teeth, going into their bedroom and putting her hair up into a bun. She preferred to wear her hair down, but while in town the day before, she hadn't seen a single woman wearing her hair down, and she knew she must conform.

She quickly dressed in a simple day dress and descended the stairs to find the children sitting at the table, and no sign of Marvin. "Where's your father?" she asked.

"He's doing the morning chores. Milking the cow and gathering eggs. Lots of days he has us do it, but he said we should wait for you."

"Well, I'm glad you did." She sat down with the children, noting that all of them sat in the same seats as they had the night before. Perhaps the children were assigned seats, but they could also just be creatures of habit. "Should I make breakfast?"

Just as she asked, Kristen came into the room with a bowl of eggs and a plate of bacon. "Coffee?" she asked Betsy in her heavily accented voice.

"Yes, please," Betsy replied.

Kristen nodded and left, returning with buttered toast and a cup of coffee. A moment later she came back with another cup of coffee and a small pitcher of milk and a bowl of sugar.

Betsy added both to her coffee, noting that the children weren't reaching for food yet. "Did you both sleep well?"

Candy nodded, but Tommy had no problem answering. "Yup. I always sleep well. Pa says it's because I play so hard, I'm asleep before my head hits the pillow."

Betsy laughed. "He's probably right."

The door opened and Betsy heard Marvin's heavy footsteps as he trod down the hall, presumably with the milk and eggs. When he came into the dining room, he was empty handed, and took his seat at the head of the table.

After a quick prayer of thanks, they all served themselves their breakfast. "Does Kristen always cook breakfast?" Betsy asked.

Marvin nodded. "She takes half a day off every Saturday, but she makes our meal before she goes."

"I can take over some of the cooking if she'd like," Betsy offered. "It would help me teach Candy to cook."

"That's not a bad idea. Maybe the two of you could cook supper on Saturday evenings. But I have no idea how we'd tell Kristen that. Her English is lacking."

"Is there anyone in your congregation fluent in both languages?" she asked.

"I think Mrs. Hansen speaks Norwegian, doesn't she?"

Candy nodded. "Ma used to talk to her in Norwegian."

"There you have it," Marvin said. "Candy can introduce you on Sunday."

"Does Kristen go to church with you?"

"She does. There's no Norwegian church, so she sits in the back with her Norwegian Bible and pretty much keeps to herself."

"I'll ask Mrs. Hansen to speak with her then."

"I'm excited to learn to cook." Candy looked very pleased.

"And to not have to go to school," Tommy said, glaring at his sister.

"You're going to school, and that's the last complaint I'll hear about it," Marvin said.

Tommy nodded. "All right."

"I want you to work with me today," Marvin said. "I need to work on fences, and I figured you could learn to fix a fence. You'll need to be able to use your hands to fix and build things."

"Yes, Pa." Tommy looked annoyed, but Betsy had a feeling he was being asked to help out with the fences so that Candy and Betsy could have time together.

After breakfast, Marvin kissed Betsy goodbye. "Be good today."

Betsy laughed. "I'm good every day."

Tommy followed his father outside, but Betsy could see he was dragging his feet. She thought it was a good idea for Tommy to learn from his father, though.

Betsy looked at Candy. "Do the men come home for lunch?"

Candy shook her head. "No, they eat at the chuck wagon with the other men."

"All right. Well, what should we do today?"

Candy shrugged. "I don't know."

"Well, do you know of any good apple trees or berry patches? Wouldn't it be fun to walk around picking some fruit? You could show me around, and we could pick fruit for a pie."

Candy smiled and nodded. "I know where we can get blackberries, blueberries, and raspberries."

"Oh, those are all wonderful in pies and jams. Are there three baskets?"

"Yes, I'll go get them."

While Candy was finding the baskets, Betsy cleared off the table, carrying the empty dishes into the kitchen. Kristen shook her head at her as she brought them in. "No."

Betsy wanted to laugh. The housekeeper was telling her what she couldn't do.

Candy and Betsy set off when she came down with the baskets. As soon as they stepped outside, Betsy shivered a bit from the chill. She'd expected the same hot weather they'd had the day before, but it was downright chilly. "Why is it so cold?"

Candy smiled. "It's always like that here. Cold at night and in the morning and hot during the day. Well, in the summer it's like that. In the winter, it's cold all the time."

"I didn't realize it would be cold. In Massachusetts if it's cold, it's cold. If it's hot, it's hot. There aren't big temperature fluctuations between different times of day."

"This is all I've ever known. But I love it here."

"I can understand why. You look out the window and see mountains. It's so beautiful."

"To me, mountains are normal. I can't imagine living somewhere without them." Candy held a basket in each hand and swung them at her sides.

Betsy smiled, watching her. "I can definitely get used to being here."

"Do you love my pa?" Candy asked, seemingly out of nowhere.

Betsy thought carefully about how to answer the question. "I can't say that I do. I just met him yesterday. I think he's very handsome and charming, and I believe I will fall in love with him quickly, but I don't love him yet."

"All right. I hope you do love him because I want you to stay."

Betsy was thrilled with the praise. "Even if I never love him, I'm staying. I promised that I would be married to him until one of us dies."

"My ma died," Candy said softly.

"I know she did. I'm so sorry."

"We had a fight the morning of the day she died. She didn't feel up to getting out of bed and she'd been sick for a very long time. I wanted her to walk me to school, and when she said she couldn't, I yelled at her and told her she was selfish. Do you think she knows I didn't mean it?"

"Oh, sweetie, of course she knows. And I know she loved you even when you were yelling. That's what mothers do. They love their children unconditionally."

"You're my new mother. Does that mean you love me?"

Betsy smiled and nodded. "Yes, it does. I choose to love you."

"But you don't choose to love Pa?"

"I do, but it's different. With romantic love, there's a little bit of something that happens between a man and a woman that's different than between a mother and daughter."

Candy nodded. "All right."

Betsy was relieved her explanation had worked for Candy. She wasn't sure what she would have said next. "Oh, I see blackberries!"

The two of them hurried toward the bush and started picking, each of them using a different basket. "I'm surprised they haven't already been picked!" They were right along the road.

"Oh, this is our land. No one will pick our berries."

Betsy pointed to the road beside them. "There are roads on your land?"

"Of course," Candy said. "There need to be roads on a ranch. This is how they get food to the chuckwagon and move the wagon around. The men sleep in a bunkhouse back there too. There are several roads here on the ranch."

"Seems like you're teaching me as much as I'm teaching you."

Candy smiled. "I like to be of help, and I love the idea of teaching you. When do we start our piano lessons?"

"We started them last night, didn't we?"

"I guess we did. It's been a long time since I've had someone to play piano with."

"I always played with my sisters. My mother insisted we all needed to know how to play."

"Did you like it?"

Betsy shrugged. "I did sometimes, and I didn't at others. I was never fond of practicing, but I'm glad I know how to play now. It will be something we can do together."

"When do I get to learn to sew?"

Betsy laughed. "You're certainly eager to learn everything. I'll talk to your pa tonight and see if he'd let us go into town and buy some fabric. I know it's a really long drive, but I think it would be nice if you could make one of your own dresses, don't you?"

"I would adore that! And there's a town where we can shop that's only a fifteen-minute drive from here. Cody is where the train station is, but we don't go there often."

"Is it where the school and church are?"

"No. They're out in the country. The store is a little further away, but if we felt very adventurous, we could walk there. It would take all day, though."

"Let's take the wagon then." Betsy loved to go for walks, but that sounded very far. "I think we've picked this one dry. Here, let me dump my berries in with yours, and then we still have two baskets for the other kinds of berries."

Chapter Five

By the time they needed to head home for lunch, Betsy and Candy had three full baskets of berries. "I'd love to teach you to make pie or jam, but I have a feeling Kristen will run us out of her kitchen if I try."

Candy giggled. "I think you're right."

"We'll just present them to her, and hopefully she'll make one or the other or both, and we'll benefit from her hard work."

"Great idea." Candy seemed happier and happier by the minute. Betsy had a feeling it had to do with not having to attend school.

"What do you think we're having for lunch?" Betsy asked.

"You never know with Kristen. Sometimes she'll make a delicious meal we want to ask her to make over and over, and sometimes she makes something that makes me want to vomit."

"When that happens, we'll sneak into the kitchen and make something for ourselves."

"I really like that plan," Candy said.

They went inside and put their baskets of berries on the kitchen table. Kristen looked at them and nodded. *"Ja ja."*

Kristen carried food into the dining room for their lunch, and Candy looked down at the plate. "I think these are a strange sandwich Kristen makes with ham and jam. They're really good, but I like your cheese sandwich better," Candy said.

Betsy sat down with Candy, and she prayed for them. "Heavenly father, thank You for this meal before us, and thank You for bringing us together. I think I've found just where I am meant to be, and I thank You for leading me here. In the name of Your son, Jesus. Amen."

Betsy took a bite of the hot sandwich. "I never would have put those things together, but this is delicious."

Candy nodded. "It's my favorite lunch she makes."

While they ate, Betsy considered the sewing lessons. "Do you know how to hitch up a wagon?" she asked Candy.

Candy shrugged. "Never done it, but it doesn't look particularly hard."

"I was hoping we could drive into town today to get your fabric, but we should probably wait until your pa is around to hitch it up."

"Probably. I don't think he'd be very happy if we tried it on our own."

"Then we'll stay here today. I have some fabric left from some aprons I made myself on the train. We could make you an apron. It would be a good project to start with."

Candy nodded. "I'd like that. We can probably talk Pa into taking us to the store on Saturday afternoon as well."

"I don't even know what day it is! I lost track on the train."

"It's Tuesday. You arrived on Monday. Did you really have to sleep sitting up on the train?"

"I did. I could have chosen a sleeper car, but that seemed needlessly expensive."

"I would have chosen a sleeper car. Wouldn't it have been nice if you could just crawl into bed and sleep whenever you wanted to?"

"I was about halfway here when I decided if I ever took a trip like that again, I would get a sleeper car." Betsy had thought she could tough it out. If she'd realized her husband was affluent, she'd have done it.

"Can we start sewing after lunch, since we can't start baking pies?"

"Absolutely. It will have to be ironed after being in my carpet bag the whole way here, but I think you need to learn to iron anyway."

Candy nodded. "Though that doesn't seem as much fun as sewing."

"I'm afraid they go hand-in-hand. You really can't sew without ironing." Betsy grinned at the girl's groan. "We'll go upstairs and get it after lunch."

"Where will we sew? Ma's sewing machine is still in the parlor, I think."

"Really? I didn't realize you had something so modern! I've used a sewing machine a few times. Mainly when I was volunteering with orphans. All of the ugliest fabrics get donated to orphans, so I would make them the prettiest dresses I could." The orphanage had made her feel like she belonged somewhere, but her mother had become concerned that she spent all of her time there, instead of strolling through town hoping to meet a man. Anything that didn't lend itself to finding a husband her mother said wasn't worth her time.

"I always watched her sew on it, but she said I needed to wait just a little longer before I was old enough. Am I old enough now?"

Betsy smiled, nodding. "I do believe you are. She probably wanted you to wait until your legs were long enough to reach the treadle."

As soon as lunch was over, Betsy went to retrieve her fabric while Candy went to make sure she knew where her mother's sewing machine was. When Betsy joined Candy, the girl was standing beside a sewing machine. "How did I miss that?" Betsy asked.

"The machine was facing down, and there was a tablecloth over the table that we had knickknacks on." Candy looked at the fabric in Betsy's hand. "Do you have a pattern?"

"Of course," Betsy said. "You'll probably want to cut yours a bit smaller than the ones I made."

"That makes sense. Now we have to iron, right?" Candy asked.

"Yes, that's next. Do you know where the iron and ironing board are?" Betsy had no idea where to even begin looking.

"I think so. I'll go look. Should I bring it in here?"

"No, I think we'll pin everything and cut it out on the table. So we'll just iron right there beside the dining table."

"Kristen is not going to like that."

Betsy laughed. "I can't spend all my time being afraid of Kristen. I know she's been here longer than me, but she's supposed to work for me, right?"

"I'm not so sure about that..." With a sassy grin, Candy hurried off to get the iron and ironing board. She came back a few minutes later with the ironing board. "Kristen did not look happy when I put the iron on the stove to heat it."

Betsy moved close to Candy and whispered, "There are two of us and only one of her. I'm sure we can beat her up!"

Candy giggled as she set up the ironing board. Betsy showed her how to get the fabric as smooth as they could without the use of the iron. "There. Now we just need the iron," Betsy said.

"You get it," Candy said.

Betsy stood straight and put her shoulders back. "I'm not afraid." She hurried into the kitchen, smiled at Kristen, took the iron, and walked serenely back into the dining room with the iron in hand.

Candy looked at her and said, "You're so brave."

The two of them laughed together as Betsy demonstrated how to iron.

After the fabric was wrinkle free, Betsy took it to the table, and she pinned the apron pattern to it. "I know I said earlier you should make yours smaller than mine, but I really think we're very close to the same size. Let's go ahead and cut it for an adult, and you'll be able to wear it for years to come."

Candy nodded. "All right."

When Betsy handed her the scissors, Candy's eyes widened. "Are you sure?"

"I'm positive. If you mess it up, we'll make something else out of it."

As she cut, Candy asked a question that Betsy struggled to find the answer for. "Are you going to have babies?"

Betsy thought for a moment. "I hope so. I've always wanted a dozen children."

"So you want twelve more, or just ten more?"

"Well, you and Tommy are my children now, so just ten more."

"Where do babies come from?" Candy was almost finished cutting when she asked that question.

"Did your mother never talk to you about this?"

Candy shook her head. "No, she always acted like it was some big secret."

"My mother did as well. When my oldest sister got married, she explained it to the rest of us, because she said we shouldn't go into marriage unprepared."

"Now you'll tell me?" Candy asked eagerly.

Uncertain if Marvin wanted Candy to have the information she was asking for or not, Betsy decided to go ahead and tell her. "I think every girl who is getting close to marriage age should know this, and I happen to know many states allow you to marry at fourteen, though I don't know if this is one of those states." She gave the girl very basic details of how a baby was made, and Candy seemed satisfied with the answer.

"Have you and Pa done that yet?"

Betsy blushed profusely. "That's not something I'm willing to talk about."

"Why not? You said it happened for the first time on a girl's wedding night, and you married Pa yesterday."

"I'm not going to discuss that with you."

Candy pouted a little, but she didn't press any further. Betsy knew she'd have to have a conversation with her at a later time about never asking anyone questions like that.

Before the men were home for supper, the apron was finished. Candy pulled it over her head and tied it behind her back. "What do you think?" she asked. "Do I look old enough to be married?"

Betsy nodded. "But I don't think a girl should marry until she's at least eighteen."

Candy groaned. "Do me a favor and don't tell Pa that."

"If your pa asks for my opinion on the matter, I will tell him. If he doesn't, I'll keep my opinion to myself. Is that fair?"

Candy nodded. "I believe it is."

The door opened then, and Tommy and Marvin came in. "Wash up, son. Supper will be on the table in a minute."

"What are you wearing?" Marvin asked Candy. "I don't think I want you looking that grown up."

He leaned down and kissed Betsy on the cheek. "Is that yours?"

Betsy shook her head. "No, she made it today."

His eyes widened in surprise. "Well, look at that. Good job, Candy!"

"Thank you, Papa. We need more fabric, but neither of us know how to hitch up the wagon."

Betsy had planned to discuss a trip to the store with Marvin, but Candy obviously wasn't feeling very patient. "Are you going to the store with Betsy?" he asked.

Candy nodded. "I need to pick out the fabric for my dress."

"Is that what you're going to make next? A dress?" he asked.

"Betsy said she'd teach me. I sewed this on Ma's sewing machine."

"I'll drive you into town in the morning," he said, glad his daughter was so eager to learn from Betsy.

"Thank you, Papa."

"I'm going to go follow my own advice and wash my hands before supper."

Kristen started setting the food on the table then. Betsy wasn't surprised to see a pie on the table, but she couldn't help but wonder which berry had been used. She still wanted to pick some apples because apple pie was her very favorite dessert.

"Pie?" Marvin asked when he came back into the room.

"Betsy and I picked three types of berries today. We had so much fun," Candy said.

"Well, I think that's wonderful. I'm glad you got some fresh air, but I'm even happier that I get to eat pie for dessert."

After their prayer, Betsy asked, "Did you enjoy working with your pa today, Tommy?"

Tommy shook his head. "All I got to do was hold out nails. Pa did all the hammering."

"And you wanted to hammer?" Betsy asked.

He nodded. "Pa said he wasn't risking either of our fingers by giving me the hammer, which I think is completely unfair."

"I tell you what," Marvin said, "You can go out and milk the cow tonight, and I'll let you do the whole job by yourself."

Candy grinned, obviously pleased her brother was going to have to do an extra chore.

"Don't look so happy, Candy," Marvin said. "I'm sending you out to collect eggs."

Candy sighed. "Yes, Pa."

Marvin looked at Betsy. "Seems as if you two had a very busy day," he said.

"Oh, we did, but it was good. We picked the berries before lunch and then we did the sewing this afternoon. We considered trying to hitch up the wagon but decided it wasn't a great idea."

"No, it wasn't. I'd rather you never hitched the wagon. It's better if you let me or one of my ranch hands do it for you. Anytime you want to go, just let me know, and we'll make it work."

Betsy smiled. "Thank you. We won't be long tomorrow. Just selecting everything we need for a brand new dress."

"I need new shoes too," Candy said. "I've outgrown these, and they're mostly worn through."

Betsy looked at Marvin, letting him make the decision. "Then get new shoes. Do you need new shoes, Tommy?"

"Of course, I do."

"Then you can ride along with us tomorrow, and we'll get you a new pair as well." Marvin looked at Betsy. "Do you need new shoes?"

Betsy smiled. "I brought six pair."

Candy's jaw dropped. "You have six pairs of shoes? Now I feel like a neglected orphan."

Marvin gave Candy his best dad look. "You will be happy with one or two pair. You can start collecting more shoes when your feet are finished growing."

"That's what you always say, Pa. I think I should be allowed two pair. One for everyday and one for church. Doesn't that sound reasonable?"

"I'll think about it," Marvin told her.

"I want to go through the children's clothes this evening, and see if there's anything else we need to add to the list of purchases. I guess I should look through yours as well."

"No, I'll let you know when I need more of something," he told her. "Focus on the children for now. And yourself if you need anything."

Betsy shook her head smiling. "My mother wouldn't have let me leave Massachusetts without everything she thought I needed. I'm set for a good long while."

Chapter Six

When they went up to bed together that evening, Betsy was very aware of how large her husband was. She knew the mechanics of lovemaking thanks to her sisters, but she couldn't imagine how it was going to work with such a big man.

When they reached their bedroom, he closed the door behind them. "I need to go into the bathroom to change into my nightgown."

He chuckled, reaching for her. "You're not going to need a nightgown."

"But I've always slept in my nightgown," she said with a frown.

"I want to feel your bare flesh against mine as we sleep."

"I...Is that all right for people to do?" she asked, genuinely having no idea whether or not he was asking her to do something that was against God.

"We're married. As long as we both enjoy it, nothing is off limits for us to do."

His hands went to the buttons at the front of her dress, and he slowly pulled them through their holes. "Wait, I should turn down the lamp."

"Why? I wouldn't be able to see you if you did!" He leaned down and nibbled at her ear, causing waves of feeling to move through her body, pooling in her stomach.

She started to ask him if it was all right if he saw her without clothing, but she knew he'd simply tell her everything was right between them as he just had.

So she stood still as he undressed her while raining kisses all over her body. Never had she imagined a man would do these things. She thought it was just get in bed, do the marriage act, and it was all over.

Marvin seemed to believe very differently than she did. Of course, he'd been married, so he would be a great deal more knowledgeable than she was.

She had no idea how long she stood there as he removed every thread of clothing she was wearing. She wanted to cover herself with her hands, or the dress that had long since fallen to the floor, but he lifted her and carried her to the bed before she could become too terribly embarrassed.

He followed her down onto the bed, and suddenly she was certain he had six hands going all over her as his mouth was glued to hers.

After a moment, he stood and his clothing went flying. "Are you always in such a hurry?" she asked.

"Not always. I'm in such a hurry because you're so beautiful!"

When he joined her on the bed this time, he cupped her face in his hands and kissed her sweetly. "Have you ever...?"

She frowned for a moment, trying to figure out what he was saying. "Oh! No, of course not. I've never been married."

He didn't tell her that people could make love without being married. He wasn't certain that was information he wanted her to have. Instead, he resumed kissing her and stroking her, moving one hand between her legs.

She gasped and arched into his hand, and he whispered, "Do you like that? You have to make sure to tell me what you do and don't like so I'll only do things you do like."

She nodded, but held her eyes tightly closed. Why did something that felt so good seem to be so wrong to her? Her mother hadn't even talked to her about this, so perhaps that was why? She promised herself then and there she wouldn't make this something her children thought was unnatural.

When Marvin moved to cover her, she wasn't thinking about her children or even about being crushed. All she could think about was the burning sensation between her legs and wanting it to stop, yet wanting to see where it would take her at the same time.

She held him tightly as he moved inside her and drove her to...she didn't know what. She just knew the feeling of having him inside her was one she'd never thought would be so delicious. She hoped they would do this often.

And then she found what she was looking for, and she arched into him, moaning softly.

He smiled as she had what he assumed was her first moment of sheer pleasure. But then he moved just like he wanted to finish off.

Afterward, he put his head on her pillow just as he had the night before. His breathing was deep and heavy, but it was the best exercise he could imagine. He'd forgotten just how good it felt to have a woman in his bed, and he promised himself, he'd never take Betsy for granted.

Finally, after he had his breath back, he said, "Want me to find my own pillow?"

She smiled. "If you'd like. There's no need for us to fight over pillows, I suppose."

"I wasn't sure if I want you to want me to stay, or if I wanted you to want me to go. It's certainly not the most comfortable way to sleep, but I very much enjoy being as close to you as I can."

"Is that what you call what we just did? Being close to each other?"

Marvin grinned. "No I call it pure heaven."

She giggled. "I never could understand why my sisters enjoyed it so much, but now...can we do that every night?"

"You will get no argument from me!"

As she snuggled down under the covers, their pillows touching and her body flush against his, she had to admit that he'd been right. There was absolutely no need for a nightgown when he was around. It would just slow him down, and now that she understood what was at the end of it all...well, she certainly didn't want to slow him down.

She fell asleep in his arms, a slight smile on her face. He may have brought her there to help Candy through her difficulties, but she was going to take advantage of being married to a strong, broad-shouldered man. Betsy was right where she belonged.

BETSY WOKE EARLIER than usual the following morning, pulling her nightgown over her head as she headed for the bathroom. Never in her dreams had she imagined feeling so good during what she and Marvin had done the night before. But now that it had happened, she couldn't imagine living without it.

She washed up and brushed her hair and teeth, returning to the bedroom to change into her day clothes. She had just pulled her corset over her head, when she heard a rustling. Marvin had his head propped up on one elbow watching her dress as if it was a show she was putting on just for him.

"Good morning," she said, not feeling at all embarrassed as she'd thought she would.

"Why'd you sneak out of bed so early? I was hoping to wake you up in a very pleasant way."

She smiled. "I'm certain we would have both enjoyed that immensely."

"So you'll come back to bed?" he asked.

She considered it, but only for a moment. "The children will be up any minute. What will they think if we're late to breakfast? One of them may feel the need to check on us!"

He sighed. "That wouldn't be good."

"No, it wouldn't. But..." She leaned down, putting her mouth right next to his ear. "I'll be thinking about what we did all day and I look forward to having you inside me again tonight."

He reached out to catch her and pull her back into bed with him, but she was too quick. "I'll see you at breakfast."

After she'd left, he lay there for a few minutes, just thinking about how very passionate she was. His first wife had put up with his attentions, but she'd never gloried in them as his sweet Betsy was doing. God had certainly smiled down on him the day she had read his letter.

By the time he'd gotten downstairs, both children and Betsy were at the table waiting for him. There was food all around. "You could have started without me," he said.

Betsy gave him a knowing look. "Now why would we do that, when I knew you were awake and about to come down to join us."

"You know, I'm not sure, but you could have started without me."

Betsy shook her head at him, and he couldn't help but laugh. "You are a minx, Betsy Small."

Candy giggled. "We need to keep her Pa. She makes us smile."

"And laugh," Marvin said. "I can't remember the last time I heard you laugh before Betsy arrived."

Candy thought about it for a moment and shook her head. "Me neither."

Betsy looked at Tommy. "We're going shopping this morning. I'm going to look through your drawers to see if there's anything you need."

Tommy sighed. "Just don't mess with my snake collection."

Betsy swallowed hard. "You have snakes in your room?"

"Just snakeskin," Marvin told her. "Nothing that will hurt you."

"All right. I'll be certain not to touch your snake collection." She looked at Candy. "Do you just want to tell me what you need, or should I go through your things as well?"

"I'll tell you what I need." Candy looked pleased that she'd been given the option and not simply been told what to do.

"And you, Mr. Small? What do you need?"

"I could use some new socks if you knit."

Betsy nodded. It was one of the things she'd learned to do for the orphans, but her mother had never let her do it at home, though the only reason she ever gave was, "We don't need to make our own garments."

"Yes, I can knit. You'll have to choose your favorite yarn colors."

"You may choose whatever you like."

"Purple it is. Maybe with some lavender flowers worked in."

Candy nodded very seriously. "Oh, yes, that sounds perfect, Betsy."

"I think so too."

"I'll choose my own colors, thank you both very much," Marvin shook his head. "I don't like that you two are picking on me together."

"We'll be a team too, Pa," Tommy said, grinning. "I know all kinds of practical jokes."

Pa smiled at Tommy. "Jokes you will not be playing on my wife and daughter. But that's all right. We can tease them just like they tease us."

In that moment, Betsy got a quite silly idea, and she decided to follow the thought. She was going to make a present for her new husband and see what he thought of it.

As soon as breakfast was over, Betsy went up the stairs and peeked into Tommy's room. She could see the snake skins, still holding the shape of the snake, and she shuddered. She didn't want to even go into his room, but Marvin walked up behind her. "They're nothing to be afraid of."

For a moment, she thought about pretending the snakes didn't bother her at all. Instead, she smiled over her shoulder at her husband. "If they're nothing to be afraid of, will you go in with me?"

Instead of laughing at her as she expected, he opened the door further and preceded her inside. Once she'd followed him, he nodded to the chest where Tommy's clothes were kept, and she went through them all carefully. "I do not believe this boy has a single item of clothing without at least one tear or stain."

Marvin shrugged. "That sounds right."

"Whole new wardrobe for Tommy then. Do you want to give me a budget to stay under?" she asked. She'd spent her entire life watching her father give her mother budgets to stick to.

He shook his head. "No, you have good judgment. If you think we need it, then you should buy it."

"All right," she said, planning to be as frugal as possible. There were a lot of things they needed, and she didn't want him to think she was a spendthrift.

When they were on the road to town just a short while later, Candy sat in the back with her brother, but she leaned against the back of the seat, talking about the kind of dress she wanted.

Once inside, they went straight to the fabric. There were some premade shirts for boys, but she didn't want to spend that much, and she enjoyed making shirts.

The men both chose yarn for their socks, and Betsy was surprised at the yarn Tommy brought her. "I want all my socks made from this," he told her.

Betsy looked at the bright red yarn in his hand. "Are you certain?"

He nodded. "And I'd love to have shirts to match."

Betsy stared at the color and nodded. "All right. There's some fabric in that color. Will khaki pants be all right?"

Tommy shrugged. "I guess. But maybe a red belt."

Betsy's eyes met Candy's and it seemed that Candy was echoing the look of sheer horror on Betsy's face. As soon as Tommy walked away, they laughed. "He will certainly stand out among his classmates," Betsy said.

Candy nodded. "I'm just glad he's not trying to find red shoes."

After finding their yarn, the men went back out to the wagon to wait while the women finished up the shopping.

It took them almost an hour to find the fabrics they wanted for the various projects they had in mind. When they did finish, the shopkeeper sent his son to carry their purchases out to the wagon.

Candy had been bubbly and excited while they shopped, until her eyes had landed on the boy, who looked to be just a little older than she was. Betsy had to wonder if she liked the boy, or if he'd done something to offend her. Of course, Candy could have simply been feeling shy. It was a side of Candy she'd rarely seen, but Betsy knew it was still there.

Betsy thought about asking about the boy while they were in the wagon headed home, but she decided to wait until they were alone together. There was no reason to upset Candy unnecessarily.

As soon as they were home, Marvin jumped down from the wagon. "Tommy will help you carry your things inside, and I'll send a ranch hand to unhitch the wagon." He strode right into the stable, and they weren't even inside the house when he rode away on a black gelding.

"I guess he hates to start work so late in the day," Betsy said, feeling a bit badly that they'd taken up some of his work time, but not too bad. She had just purchased a lot of work for herself. Now she wouldn't feel lazy as Kristen did all the work around the house.

"Just put it all in the parlor," Betsy told Tommy.

"You'll start on my socks first?" Tommy asked.

"I'll work on them whenever your sister can work on her own for a bit."

Candy smiled. "I think he wants those red socks."

"I guess he does."

Chapter Seven

Betsy and Candy spent the whole day in the parlor, with Candy sewing and Betsy knitting red socks. When Candy had a question, Betsy would set down the socks, and the two of them would work together for a few minutes, but Tommy was running into the house to check on the progress made on his socks too often for them to really spend time working on anything together.

"Maybe you should teach me to knit, and I can work on socks as well. I don't think we'll get anything done until Tommy has red socks on his feet," Candy suggested.

Betsy smiled. "I'll teach you to knit, but not today. I have to hurry to make these before Tommy's feet fall off because they're not wearing them!"

Candy giggled. "I don't know why he suddenly needs to have red socks."

"And a red shirt to match. I think I can have the socks done by supper. I'm a competent knitter, and pretty fast, so it won't take too much. Then tomorrow, while you sew, I'll work on cutting out a red shirt for him."

"I think he wants two red shirts."

"Then I'll make him two red shirts if that's what he wants. Has he ever cared about what he wore before?" Betsy was baffled at the boy's interest in red socks and a red shirt. It simply didn't seem like him.

Candy shook her head. "No, he used to refuse to wear socks or shoes. In fact, I don't think he wore socks all last year. Even in the winter, when his feet had to be freezing."

"It's a mystery, I suppose." With the orphans she'd worked with back home, she hadn't had a single boy under the age of fifteen who was interested in what he wore. None of them even cared if they wore shirts that were torn and patched a hundred times.

"Can you show me how to baste this properly? It didn't matter too much with the apron, but I'll wear this in public."

"Yes, you will. And it will be beautiful."

Ten minutes later when Tommy walked into the house, he saw Betsy working with Candy on her dress again. "You're never going to make those socks, are you?"

Betsy laughed. "I'll have them done before supper. Your sister has questions as she sews, but your socks will get done."

Tommy looked skeptical. "Show me."

Betsy rolled her eyes, but she found the sock she had finished, and showed him the one she had just started. "Happy now?" she asked.

Tommy thought about it for a moment. "Not yet. When the socks are done, I'll be happy."

"Why red socks?" Betsy asked.

"To match my red shirt."

"Why do you want a red shirt?"

"To match my red socks of course." Tommy shook his head in exasperation. "Girls get confused so easily."

"I know less now than I did before I asked," Betsy said when he'd left the house.

"And girls get confused? I swear, he cannot be my brother." Candy returned to her sewing, understanding a little better what she was doing, while Betsy got back to the socks. The red socks. The ones Tommy needed to match his red shirt, which he needed to match his red socks. It made no sense whatsoever.

"I'll ask your pa," Betsy said. "Maybe he'll know what's going through Tommy's head."

"I like to think my pa is too smart to even try to understand Tommy."

Kristen poked her head into the parlor. "Cookies?"

"Oh, yes, please!" Candy said. "Come on Betsy."

"We can't eat them in here?" Betsy asked.

"If we eat them anywhere but the table, we'll get fussed at in Norwegian, and I kind of worry what she's saying to us."

Betsy got to her feet, setting the socks on the sofa. "I guess we'll eat at the table then. She said cookies very well in English. Are we sure she doesn't understand?"

Candy nodded. "She can say cake, cookies, supper, and various other food words. She doesn't understand much else though."

At the table, Kristen had three glasses of milk and a plate of cookies, as well as three small plates. "Tommy?" she asked.

"I'll get him." Candy ran to the door and shouted her brother's name at the top of her lungs. "Tommy! Cookies!"

Candy returned to the table, and served herself three of the cookies from the plate in the middle of the table.

"Are you sure he's coming?" Betsy asked.

The front door banged into the wall, and Tommy ran into the dining room, skidding to a halt beside the table. "Cookies!"

"Wash your hands first," Betsy said without even thinking.

When Tommy returned, he sat down and grabbed four cookies from the plate. "This is just what I needed. Shopping takes a lot out of a boy."

"Maybe running around outside like a small tornado is what takes a lot out of a boy?" Betsy asked.

Tommy seemed to consider that. "Nah, it's the shopping."

Betsy worried that she didn't have the same rapport with Tommy as she did with Candy, but Tommy didn't seem to need her as much as Candy did. He was happy as long as he could do what he wanted.

While they ate, Tommy talked about how much he wanted a pink chicken. "I think all chickens should be pink," he announced. "Do you think I could paint one of the chickens pink?"

"I really don't think that's a good idea," Betsy said, acting as if it was a question she heard every day.

"That's too bad. All our chickens are boring white, but my friend Bobby has chickens that are different colors. I want ours to be like his."

"Perhaps I could talk to your father about buying two of Bobby's family's chickens or trading two of ours for two of theirs."

Tommy looked excited. "Oh, would you?"

"I don't know why not," Betsy told him. He wanted things that seemed strange to her, but she was certain he would feel the same about things she wanted.

After Tommy hurried back outside, Kristen came in and removed the cookies from the table, shooing Betsy and Candy away.

"What's that about?"

"Oh, she likes Tommy best," Candy said. "He's the only reason she made the cookies, but she's not so mean that she won't share them with all of us."

"Has she always liked Tommy best?" Betsy asked. That didn't seem very fair to Candy in her opinion.

"Oh, yes. It's okay though. I don't mind."

"All right." Betsy thought the entire thing was odd, but she knew it wouldn't do much good to tell Candy that. She wasn't quite sure why Kristen was still there when she couldn't speak to anyone.

Just before supper, Betsy finished the second sock. She held them up beside one another to make sure they looked even and straight, and that's when Tommy came barreling into the room.

"They're done! They're done!" He took them out of Betsy's hands and sat down, removing his shoes and what appeared to Betsy to be the dirtiest, holiest socks in the known world.

Throwing the socks in the middle of the floor, he said, "You can throw those away if you want. I'll never wear socks that aren't red again. Can you make more?"

Betsy nodded. "I'm sure I can."

"These are perfect!" Tommy said. "Oh, I'm the happiest boy in the world!" He threw his arms around Betsy and kissed her cheek. "Thanks, Ma."

Marvin stepped into the doorway at that moment. "Well, look at those socks." He seemed as perplexed about the obsession with red socks as Betsy felt.

"Aren't they wonderful, Papa? I want ten more pair just like them! And three red shirts!"

"Three?" Betsy asked. "I'm not sure if I have enough fabric for three. I know I have enough for two, and I'll do my best to make three out of it."

"Good idea," Tommy said. "Make my first shirt next. I won't even feel the need to wear pants since my socks will match my shirt!" He hurried out of the parlor.

"I'll talk to him later," Marvin said. "We don't want to get another note from the teacher about him taking his pants off in class."

Another? Betsy decided she would never ask about the first note. No, it simply wasn't a good idea. "I think supper's ready," she said.

"Smart woman," Marvin said. "Always best not to understand."

When Betsy walked into the dining room, she saw Kristen exclaiming excitedly over the red socks Tommy wore. The words she spoke weren't in English, but Tommy seemed thrilled that she was paying attention to him and acting as excited about the socks as he felt.

Supper was already on the table, and Betsy sent Marvin and Tommy to wash their hands. Having caught a glimpse of Tommy's leg when he changed his socks, she had a feeling the boy hadn't bathed in at least a month. That was going to have to change. School was starting, and though Tommy hadn't had a mother for three years, he had one now, and he was not going to school filthy.

While they ate, Candy talked about how excited she was to be making a dress for herself. "Now that Tommy's socks are finished, perhaps he won't come inside every ten minutes and scold Betsy for not knitting fast enough."

Marvin's eyes were filled with amusement as he listened to every word his daughter said raptly. "It sounds like you're already learning a lot."

"So much more than I would at school!" Candy said.

"But you will be doing your regular schoolwork," Marvin said. "You're such a smart girl. I don't want you to fall behind your classmates."

"We'll work that out," Betsy said. "I think we'll do her book learning in the mornings, and then we'll spend the afternoon sewing or knitting or cooking or cleaning. There are so many things she wants to learn."

"Well, I'm glad you're thinking about that. I worry you two will enjoy doing the other things so much you'll forget your book learning."

"It's not going to happen," Betsy said. "No matter how much both of us would prefer it."

"Pa?" Tommy said.

"Yes?"

"Do you think the chickens will like my new red socks?"

Marvin drew his brows together. Betsy could see him trying to understand how to answer the question. "Well, son, I'm not sure if chickens like socks at all, but if they do, I'm sure they like red socks best."

"Can I paint one of the chickens pink? Ma said it's not a good idea, but I think they'd look better pink, don't you?"

"I don't think chickens like paint, so that's not going to work."

"My friend Bobby has silkie chickens, and they're pink. Can we buy some pink chickens from them? Please, Pa?" Tommy seemed so earnest that it was all Betsy could do not to laugh. Marvin seemed to know how to handle Tommy most of the time, but his off-the-wall desires were confusing.

"I'll talk to Bobby's pa at church on Sunday. They may not want to give up any pink chickens." Marvin kept his face serious as he spoke. Betsy was very impressed.

"I wonder if pink chickens lay pink eggs," Candy said. "Pink eggs would be awful pretty."

Betsy had no idea why Tommy was as obsessed with the things he was, but she didn't mind. He was calling her Ma after all. It was so good to hear the word and know it was about her.

After supper, they went back to the parlor, where they had cleaned up their sewing mess before the men came in for supper. "Can we play the piano tonight?" Candy asked.

Betsy looked over at Marvin for an answer. If he didn't mind, she would happily work with Candy. If not, they could do something else.

"You know what? You spend a lot more time with my wife than I do. Why don't we go for a nice long walk?" Marvin didn't have a ton of energy after working all day, but he thought it would be good to walk with Betsy and the children.

Betsy and Candy looked at each other. "Can we take baskets and pick berries?" Candy asked.

Marvin smiled. "Why don't we just walk tonight, and you two can pick berries tomorrow if you'd like."

"We should wait another week," Betsy suggested. "That way we can have a lesson in jam-making."

Candy smiled. "Great idea."

As they all traipsed out of the house for their after supper walk, Marvin reached out to take Betsy's hand. She felt a little uncomfortable about the display of affection with the children watching, but she decided they needed to get used to it. She had no plans to go anywhere.

Candy walked on one side of Betsy and Marvin on the other, leaving Tommy to run ahead and pick up rocks and everything else he could see. He'd find something of great interest to his nine-year-old mind and bring it back to show them. Once it was a rock, he was certain was gold. Then it was a feather. Lastly, he found a bird's nest on the ground.

"Can you put it back up in the tree, Pa?"

"I'm not sure about that, son."

"Please, Pa?"

Marvin nodded and walked to the tree, reaching up and putting it onto a branch up against the trunk. "I hope the birds find their house and move back in," he said to Tommy.

"Me too! We should make a bunch of nests and put them in all the trees!" Tommy suggested.

Betsy smiled. "I don't know, Tommy. You know how much you liked choosing the color for your socks?"

Tommy nodded. "Yeah..."

"Don't you think the birds like their homes a certain way?" Betsy asked. "They may like some twigs better than others, and since we can't be sure, we should let them build their own homes."

Tommy thought about it for a moment before nodding. "Yes, we should. I want to do something nice for them, though."

Marvin nodded. "I have an idea. Let's build a birdhouse. Then they can come in out of the rain so they don't get wet."

"Do you know how to build a birdhouse, Pa?"

"Of course, I do. I used to make them and sell them when I was your age. I painted them all kinds of fun colors."

"Can we paint them pink?"

Marvin nodded. He didn't understand his son all the time, but he knew they wouldn't hear the end of it if they didn't have a pink birdhouse.

Soon, after, they turned around. "I wish we could go further, but it's starting to get dark, and that means it's bedtime."

Betsy felt a warmth wash through her body at the idea of bedtime. Now that she knew what to expect, she looked forward to it.

Chapter Eight

The following morning, Betsy woke to a hand cupping her breast, and a mouth against her ear whispering, "Wake up."

She smiled and turned to Marvin, her arms going around him. "But it's not even dawn yet."

"If we wait til dawn, we'll have to wait til tonight, and my life will be over!"

She giggled. "You're so melodramatic!"

He hushed her up by applying his mouth to hers.

A while later, after dawn, Betsy went down the hall to wash up. She dearly wanted a bath, but she wanted the water to be hot enough to get the filth off Tommy, and the boy was going to bathe right after breakfast. It was time, and everyone but Tommy knew it.

Once dressed, she went to sit at the table for breakfast, seeing only the children there. "Is your pa doing the morning chores?" she asked.

Candy nodded, but she seemed extremely distracted.

Deciding she would deal with Candy later, she turned to Tommy. "Guess what you get to do after breakfast?"

"Try on more socks!"

"No, you get to take a bath! You will use soap and wash yourself all over!"

"But, Ma! I hate taking baths!"

"I'm not making you any more clothes until you're clean. No red shirts and no more socks." Betsy had no idea where the threat had come from, but it made her feel as if she was a real mother as soon as it slipped out.

"Fine, I'll take a bath, but I refuse to like it!"

"You need a boat for the tub. Then you'll like it."

"No, I won't!" Tommy pouted.

The look on Marvin's face as he walked into the dining room told Betsy he'd heard a lot of the conversation. "Listen to your mother," was all he said.

"Can you make a boat for Tommy for the next time I'm mean to him and force him to bathe?" Betsy asked sweetly.

"I think I can do that. Should be easy enough to carve a boat from wood."

Tommy said nothing, but Betsy was certain he would come up with a color he wanted it painted soon.

Candy said nothing the whole while they ate, and after breakfast, while Tommy took his bath, Betsy went into the parlor with Candy. "What's wrong?" she asked.

"I'm dying." Candy's words were more matter of fact than dramatic.

"Why? What is wrong?"

"I'm bleeding between my legs. I'm sure I'm dying."

"Oh! Did no one talk to you about your cycle?"

"My cycle? I've always wanted a bicycle, but Pa thinks they're just for boys."

Betsy patiently explained what was "wrong" with Candy. "It happens to all women. It just means you're growing up."

"But...why didn't anyone tell me?" Candy wailed.

"Your mother would have, and your grandmother sounds like she wasn't going to answer any questions about those things. So I get to be the one to tell you."

Candy sighed. "Sometimes I really wish my ma was here to talk to me."

"I'm so sorry she's not. I'll do the best I can to help you through these things, but I can never truly replace your mother." Betsy put her arm around Candy's shoulders and Candy all but melted into her side. "I have some special cloths to use, and I'll give them to you as soon as your brother is done with his bath."

"Thank you."

By the time Tommy came down from his bath, Betsy and Candy had cut out his shirt together. Betsy gave Candy what she needed and explained how to use the clothes, giving her safety pins as well before going back downstairs to start basting Tommy's shirt together.

Candy seemed much happier when she came back downstairs, and she worked on her dress at the sewing machine, while Betsy gave her attention to the shirt.

Thankfully, Tommy wasn't running inside every few minutes to check her progress on the shirt.

They took turns at the machine. When Candy needed to do something away from the machine, Betsy used it and vice versa. It worked out very well sewing together. And by suppertime, both the dress and the shirt were finished. Betsy knew Tommy would be over the moon about his shirt, so she put it on the back of the chair he sat in at the table.

When he walked into the house, he squealed. "My red shirt!"

"You took a bath, so I made the shirt."

Tommy reached toward the shirt.

"Stop!" Betsy said. "That's a brand-new clean shirt. Don't you think your hands should be clean before you touch it?"

Tommy grunted, but he went to the kitchen to wash his hands, talking up a storm to Kristen the whole while. Betsy couldn't help but wonder how close they'd be if they actually spoke the same language.

BY THE TIME THE FIRST day of school rolled around, Betsy had made five pairs of red socks and three red shirts. She'd had to be creative with the cutting, but she'd been able to get all three out of the initial piece of fabric she'd purchased.

She found she was very nervous about teaching Candy and making sure she stayed caught up with her peers, in case she ever wanted to return to school.

Tommy wore his new socks with the matching shirt, and he strutted out the door as if he was king of the world. Marvin drove Tommy to school while Betsy and Candy set up the dining room table as their schoolroom.

They started with arithmetic because Candy said it was her most hated subject. It was easier to get it over with.

They worked at school until noon, and then ate their lunch. "I thought today we'd do two different subjects for the afternoon," Betsy told her new student.

"Which ones?" Candy asked eagerly.

"We're going to pick some berries and make jam," Betsy said. "And then, if there's time, we will have a piano lesson. Kristen said we could use the kitchen for three hours, but we have to get out of her way so she can make supper."

Candy nodded. "Did you have Mrs. Hansen talk to her?"

"I did. And we get to cook supper on Saturdays."

"Oh, good. I was hoping that would work out. I'm excited to make my first meal!"

Betsy smiled. "Good. This is going to work well for us, I think."

Once the berries were picked, they went into the kitchen and got everything prepared for the jam they were going to make. They had a variety of berries they'd picked and decided to experiment with them. They decided to just put them all in the same pot and see how the jam turned out. The berries were quickly going out of season, but they could pick more if they didn't like how this turned out.

Betsy taught Candy how to measure and how to properly stir the pot, digging deep and making sure they scraped the bottom and sides.

They canned all the jam except for a small amount they kept out to eat with breakfast the following morning.

MAIL ORDER MAGNIFICENCE

As soon as it was cool, they each took a taste with a spoon.

Candy took her bite and grinned. "This is delicious. We did a great job!"

"Did you doubt we would?"

"Not really. You seem to be good at everything."

Betsy smiled. "I wouldn't have come here expecting to do all the cooking, cleaning, and sewing if I hadn't been sure I could do it."

"Pa says you're magnificent. I agree. You're the best substitute mother I could possibly ask for." Candy threw her arms around Betsy and held her tight. "Thank you!"

"For what?" Betsy asked.

"For teaching me at home. For not giving up and heading home when you met me and I didn't speak to you. For being you."

Betsy felt a tear pop into her eye. "Back east, I lived with my parents and four sisters. The worst part about the sisters is we all have the same color hair. Each of us has a different eye color, but no one ever noticed really. All of my sisters were wonderful at something. And I was just me. So people would see me and say, 'She's just another O'Brien sister.' I never really had my own identity. Then I came here, where no one knows me, and no one knows my sisters. I was as quiet as you are in Massachusetts. Here I finally feel as if I have my own identity."

"So you were like me?"

"In a lot of ways, I was. My mother sent me to finishing school, but she didn't send any of my sisters. Mother said I was the one who needed to find who she was meant to be. All my sisters already knew."

Candy frowned. "Did you make friends there?"

"No, I never did. I was miserable. I'd never really had a friend, and I didn't know how to make one. Everything is so much better for me here."

"I hope I don't have to move across the country so I can feel valued," Candy said.

"You are very valued. By your pa, your brother, and me. I can't imagine life without you anymore."

Candy smiled. "Let's go do that piano lesson."

Betsy could almost see Candy filling up with confidence after their talk. It was as if she needed to realize there were other people like her in the world, and she was just fine the way she was.

When Tommy came in from school, he hurried to the parlor. "Everyone loves my new socks and shirts. The teacher said she hoped they'd make me behave better."

Betsy bit her lip. "And did they?"

"Probably not. I'm going to change into play clothes so I don't mess up my new shirt." He ran from the room, and they could hear him as he thundered up the stairs.

"I didn't even get to ask him about his first day of school."

"There's always supper," Candy responded.

They decided to serve the jam they'd put into the ice box with supper. Kristen was making something with biscuits as a side, and Betsy thought the jam would be delicious on the biscuits.

Candy put the jam on the table just before the prayer was said.

When Marvin took a biscuit, she nudged the jam toward him. "Betsy and I made it," she said.

"Then I'll have to try it, won't I?"

He smiled when he took his first bite. "What kind of berry did you use?"

Candy giggled. "Blueberry, blackberry, raspberry, and elderberry."

"Well, all I can say is it's delicious. I want to eat it every day."

Betsy smiled. "Good, because we made twelve jars. We could probably pick a few more berries and make another batch."

Tommy held out his hand. "Let me try it."

Betsy watched him. He was the pickiest eater she'd ever met, so she knew if he liked it, they'd done a good job.

He slowly spread it on his biscuit and took one tiny bite. She didn't know how it was even enough to know that he liked it, but he took a bigger bite immediately. "This is good. Make more."

Candy giggled. "I guess it's really good if it passed the Tommy test."

"I want jam sandwiches for lunch tomorrow," Tommy said. "I'll go and tell Kristen." He jumped up from the table and was gone before anyone had time to respond to him.

When he came back, he finished his biscuit before saying, "She's going to send the jam sandwiches."

"How did you tell her what you want?" Betsy asked curiously.

"I pointed to a jar of jam, and then to bread, and then to my lunch pail. Simple."

"Do you talk to her a lot that way?"

"Oh, sure," Tommy said. "I told her to make cookies too."

"I see. Does she always do what you want?"

"Yup. She likes me best."

"And how do you know that?" Betsy asked.

"Everyone knows that," Tommy replied. "She makes my favorite cookies all the time, and she never makes anything I don't like again. No more lutefisk."

Betsy decided the next time she had to try to communicate with Kristen, she would do the same. She felt sorry for the older woman. She spent all her time with people she couldn't communicate with. "What does she do on Saturdays?"

"Her sister and her family live in Casper. Someone hitches the wagon for her after lunch, and she drives there and spends the evening with her. Sometimes she's not home until right before time to make breakfast."

"I had no idea she had family so close. Why doesn't she live with her sister?"

"From what she told Lynn, she tried to live with her, but her husband seemed to think Kristen was his property. So they decided she would stay near enough to visit, but not near enough to live there. She dotes on her sister's grandchildren from what I understand."

"It sounds like it's best that she's here then. I do wish I could communicate with her without having to bother Mrs. Hansen though," Betsy said.

"Just take Tommy with you when you want to talk to her. He can interpret."

"I'm not so certain he can," she said, shaking her head.

"I can," Tommy said. "She understands me when I point and do stuff like that, and I understand her gibberish."

"You understand Norwegian?" Betsy asked, surprised.

Tommy nodded. "I can't answer her, but I understand her."

"I think that's wonderful," Betsy said with a smile. "Maybe we can talk to her together."

"Maybe."

"How was the first day of school?" Marvin asked.

Tommy shrugged. "It was good, but the teacher stopped me when I tried to take my pants off. I was just showing everyone that my socks and shirt match. I don't know why she was so uptight about it." He gave his attention to his food while his father closed his eyes.

"I don't know what to do with you sometimes, Tommy," Marvin said.

"I guess you just have to love me the way I am."

Marvin turned his attention to his daughter. "And how was your first day of school?"

"It was wonderful! We did our bookwork in the morning and then we picked berries, made jam, and had a piano lesson."

"That sounds like a very good day," Marvin said. "I'm glad you're feeling comfortable as you learn."

Candy nodded. "I'm just glad we have a Betsy now. What would we do without her, Pa?"

He looked at his wife and smiled. "I have no clue at all."

Betsy was embarrassed, but it was a good embarrassed, not like the time the back of her dress had been caught in her bloomers, and she'd walked into school that way.

"I'm glad you're all so fond of me!" she finally said. "I'm not going anywhere."

Chapter Nine

By early November, Candy was able to speak with others at church without having Betsy right beside her. Betsy was quite proud of the work they'd been able to do, and she was willing to keep on for a while, but she thought it would be better if Candy went back to school, to spend time with her peers.

One Sunday after church, Betsy was in the parlor crocheting a red scarf and red hat for Tommy for Christmas. Betsy was alone, which was becoming more and more common these days.

There was enough snow on the ground that Tommy was out with his friend Bobby, and they were sledding. Marvin was out finding some cattle who had been separated from the herd when they moved them on Saturday.

Candy joined Betsy in the parlor. "That's coming along well," Candy said, looking at the scarf in Betsy's hand.

Betsy smiled. "I do think Tommy will like it."

"I do too. And he won't feel the need to take his pants off during school to show everyone how well it all matches."

Betsy shook her head. "I hope not. Miss Andrews and I are becoming quite good friends thanks to all the meetings she needs to have with me."

"I think that may be why Grandmother left when she did. She said something about never going to another meeting with the teacher again."

"Do you miss your grandmother?"

Candy shook her head. "Not at all. She was always angry about something. She yelled at Kristen for being late with breakfast one morning. It wasn't good having her here."

"I'm sorry it wasn't a better experience for you." Betsy had been very close to her father's mother, who had taught her many things. Her mother had gotten angry when she found out Betsy was learning to cook and sew, so she'd stopped letting Betsy spend time with her.

"It doesn't matter. Everything is better now that you're here."

Betsy smiled, and covered Candy's hand with hers. "I'm happy to be here."

"I know." Candy took a deep breath. "You know that boy I told you about? The one I have a crush on?"

"Yes." Candy had talked more about him every week, and Betsy knew they were spending time talking together before and after church. "What about him?"

"He asked me to the church social on Saturday night. Pa said all decisions about Tommy and me are going to be handled by you... So, may I go?"

Betsy smiled. "I think that would be good. You can really get to know Steven better that way."

"I hope so," Candy said. "I want to marry him."

Betsy's eyes widened. "You need to be older to marry him."

"I do?" Candy asked. "I know a girl who got married at fourteen, and she's really happy."

"Well, you're not quite fourteen yet, but I think it's better to wait to marry until you're at least eighteen."

"Eighteen? That's still over four years away!" Candy shook her head. "Eighteen seems so old."

"It's not though," Betsy said. "You'll have just finished school and be ready to move on to the next portion of your life. If you were married, you'd have to stop going to school."

"I'm sure Pa will let me marry at fourteen. He won't mind."

"That's between you and your pa then. I'm not making that decision for you."

"But I can still go to the church social, right? Steven asked me to send a note with Tommy tomorrow if you say yes."

Betsy nodded. "I think the church social is perfectly appropriate."

"I'm going to work on the scarf I'm making for Pa," Candy said, going to the corner of the room and getting her yarn and crochet hook.

While they worked, they talked about what they wanted to take for their contribution to the church social. Everyone was bringing everything to share.

"We could take a cake or cookies?" Candy suggested.

"There are always more desserts than meals though. Maybe we could make a pot pie? Chicken or beef?"

"Now that Tommy has chickens of his own, he gets really upset when we butcher a chicken for a meal," Candy reminded Betty. "He thinks it scares his chickens."

Betsy sighed. "You're right. We'll make it a beef pot pie."

"And I can bake some cookies as well!" Candy said excitedly.

"That sounds good to me," Betsy said. "Then we're each making a contribution."

"Can I make a new dress for the social?" Candy asked. "We have that green fabric we bought, and we never got around to making a dress for me with it."

"We can do that," Betsy said. She knew how important it was for a young girl to go out with a boy for the first time. Of course, her own first kiss had been with Marvin, but her sisters had talked about their courtships with her. She was the only one who listened. "We'll cut it out tomorrow afternoon."

"Oh, thank you, Betsy! You're the best mother a girl could ask for!"

At supper that evening, Candy talked about the dress she wanted to make for the social the following weekend. Marvin smiled and nodded, but Betsy could see he wasn't listening to his daughter.

Tommy frowned. "I need a new red shirt if she's getting a new dress."

"You already have five red shirts," Betsy told him. "Why could you possibly need more?"

"I just...well, I like new red shirts."

Marvin sighed. "You can wear one of the red shirts your ma has already made for you."

"But all my friends have seen those red shirts before, and Candy is wearing something new."

Marvin looked at Betsy for help. "I could make you some red mittens to wear. Would that be good?"

Tommy's face lit up. "Red mittens! They'll match my socks and shirts!"

"They will," Betsy said. It was a very good thing she enjoyed knitting.

"Thanks, Ma!"

After supper, they all gathered in the parlor. Tommy had his fleet of boats he was pushing around on the floor. Betsy and Candy were both working on projects. Candy had decided to make a pair of socks for Steven for Christmas, and she was already working on them. And Betsy was back to knitting with the red yarn Tommy favored.

Marvin sat whittling yet another boat for Tommy. After he'd gotten the first one, he'd decided that he needed several boats, so he could have the unpainted ones crash into the pink ones.

When Betsy went into the bathroom after Tommy had bathed, there was water everywhere. It took two towels to clean up the entire mess. But Tommy was bathing twice a week now, instead of the once per month he preferred. As far as Betsy was concerned, he could have all the toy boats and make all the messes he wanted, as long as he was taking baths.

They all talked about the weather, and what they wanted to do for Christmas. "Can we have a tree inside this year?" Candy asked. "Like we used to have when Ma was alive?"

"We can if you'd like that," Marvin said.

"We'll string popcorn!" Betsy said.

"We have a few ornaments I got from a catalog," Marvin said. "I'll get those out, and maybe we can order a few more."

"And you can carve a train for under the tree this year, Papa?" Tommy asked.

"And why do we need a train under the tree?" Marvin asked.

"How else will all the presents get from one place to another?"

"I guess you're right."

"We're going caroling again, right?" Candy asked.

"We always do," Marvin said. "This year we'll have Kristen have some hot chocolate and cookies waiting for us when we get home."

"We were so cold last year," Tommy said.

For a moment, Betsy was sad she hadn't been part of all those memories with her family, but just as she had a history before them, they had one before her.

"I need more boats," Tommy announced after a moment of silence.

Marvin's eyes widened. "Exactly how many boats am I going to carve for you, son?"

Tommy shrugged. "A hundred sounds good."

"I'm sure it does sound good to you," Marvin said shaking his head.

"I should make a shawl to go with my dress!" Candy suggested.

"You're going to need a coat. It'll be too cold on Saturday for just a shawl."

"I guess..." Candy said, but Betsy could see she was still thinking about making a shawl.

THE NEXT FEW DAYS PROVED to be very difficult for Betsy. She woke up sick the following morning, unable to keep her breakfast down. But by noon, she felt perfectly fine.

MAIL ORDER MAGNIFICENCE

Candy had progressed enough with her sewing that she didn't need much help, but Betsy still had to make mittens by Saturday evening. It wasn't a difficult project, but everything seemed overwhelming that day.

Tommy had left that morning with a note for Steven in his lunch pail. When he returned with a note from Steven, Candy read it excitedly. "He and his parents will be here to fetch me at five thirty on Saturday evening."

Betsy smiled. "I'm glad you're looking forward to it so much."

At supper, Candy told her pa that she'd be going to the church social with Steven and his family.

Marvin put his fork down and stared at his daughter. "I don't want you courting until you're at least fifteen. I know I've told you that before."

"But Betsy said I could go with him."

Marvin glared at Betsy for a moment before focusing his attention on his daughter. "I know you want to go, but you should have asked me."

"But, Pa! You said all decisions about Tommy and me should be made by Betsy. So I spoke to Betsy, got her permission, and sent a note for Steven with Tommy to school saying I'd go. I can't go back on my word."

"It's not going back on your word if you never got permission in the first place," Marvin told her.

"But I did get permission. I already told you that!"

"Betsy should have come to me before agreeing, and I'll talk to her about that later. For now, I need you to write another note to Steven and tell him your pa is not going to let you go to the church social with him or any other boy until you're at least fifteen."

"By then, he'll be taking Anna to all the church socials!" Candy got up and ran from the table up to her room, leaving everyone in silence.

Tommy finished eating. "I'm going to go take a bath with my boats," he said.

Betsy nodded, making a mental note he was bathing on Monday evening. Then she could know when to prompt him to take a bath again, though lately, he hadn't needed that prompting.

As soon as he'd run off, Marvin glared at Betsy. "What were you thinking telling her she could go without even consulting me?"

Betsy wanted to cry. It was the first time she'd told one of the children they could do something and he hadn't been agreeable. "I did tell her not to think of marriage until she's eighteen."

"Marriage? You talked to my daughter about when she could marry?"

"I thought she was our daughter," Betsy said with a voice that was very soft compared to Marvin's yelling.

"She is...but her father needs to have a say in these things."

"Her father acted like he didn't care what she does." Betsy knew the words were harsh, but so were his. She wanted to run off and lick her wounds.

"I see. From now on, I would appreciate it if you came to me on decisions about my daughter dating and didn't just make them yourself."

"What about your son? What if he wants to court someone? Do I come to you then?" she asked.

"It's different with a boy."

"Excuse me? So, if Tommy wanted to take someone to the social on Sunday, that would be acceptable, even though he's four years younger?" Betsy could feel anger building inside her. She no longer wanted to lick her wounds. She wanted to break her supper plate over his head.

He shrugged. "I don't have to worry about Tommy getting himself pregnant."

"And you don't have to worry about Candy getting herself pregnant either! First of all, she can't get herself pregnant. It takes two. Secondly, she has better morals than that. She comes to me with all the thoughts that go through her head. Yes, she likes this boy, but she would go with him and his family. They wouldn't be alone at all!"

He stood up. "I'm not listening to this anymore. Since you were the one who told her she could go with Steven, you can tell her she can't." He left the dining room, and she heard the front door slam.

Lovely. Now her husband was angry with her. Her daughter hated her. Tommy was too busy with his boats to care about the drama at the dining room table. And she had to throw up again. The perfect ending to a less than perfect day.

She changed into her nightgown and waited for Tommy to emerge from the bathroom. There she splashed cold water on her face and rinsed out her mouth.

On her way back to her room for bed, she knocked on Candy's door. "It's me," she called.

"Go away!"

Betsy opened the door and walked inside, sitting on the side of Candy's bed, where she lay face down, her face buried in a pillow.

"I'm going to keep working on your pa," Betsy said.

Candy rolled to her side. "You are?"

"I am. I think he's being unreasonable. So I will talk to him more after he's calmed down a little." Betsy's hand covered her stomach as she spoke, knowing she would have to run any second.

"Are you sick again?" Candy asked, looking concerned.

Betsy nodded, jumped up, and ran for the bathroom. After rinsing her mouth once more, she returned to Candy. "Sorry about that."

"You can't be sorry for being sick," Candy said. "I won't allow it."

Betsy laughed softly. "I just felt like I ran away mid-conversation, and that's rude."

"I did the same at supper. Don't worry about it!" Candy hugged her stepmother. "Thank you for trying to help Pa understand how unreasonable he is."

"I can't make any promises other than I will do my very best. Which is what I've always done for you."

"I know you have. Thank you!"

Betsy said goodnight, and headed back to her room, all but falling into bed. The lamp still lit. She was much too tired to care about anything else that night, and she fell asleep quickly.

Marvin walked into their room an hour later, ready for another fight, but what he found was his wife already sleeping. Instead of fighting with her, he undressed, turned down the lamp, and got into bed beside her. She looked so sad and innocent in her sleep. And he loved every second that he spent with her.

Chapter Ten

Betsy woke and headed straight for the bathroom the following morning. Again, she was sick.

She went back to her room and crawled back into bed.

Marvin looked over at her. "You're still sick, aren't you?"

"Yes, and I never get sick. I cannot remember the last time I threw up, and here I am, sick for two days straight. I'm making sure I still teach Candy and working on Tommy's socks though. I won't shirk my duties."

All at once Marvin felt guilt wash over him. She was this ill, and all he'd done was yell at her the night before. She hadn't deserved that. "I think we should let Candy go to the church social with Steven and his family," he said softly.

"You do?"

He didn't, but he felt he needed to apologize somehow, and this was the only way he could think of. "They'll be with his parents, and I'm sure they'll keep an eye on the two of them."

"Oh, thank you!" Betsy said. "I just know Candy is going to be so happy you made that decision." She sat up and threw her arms around him, realizing too late that was a huge mistake. She ran for the bathroom without a word to him, but he'd seen the look on her face.

When she returned, he said, "I'm going for the doctor today. He'll ride out and check you over. I'm worried about you."

"Oh, there's no need to worry. People get sick stomachs for any number of reasons." And then it dawned on her. She hadn't had a cycle since she'd left Massachusetts. How could she be so dense? She started to tell him what she thought but stopped herself. She wanted to have a doctor confirm it before she said anything. "Maybe I should see the doctor after all."

"I'll ride into town right after breakfast."

She clutched her stomach. "Just the thought of food makes me sick. I definitely need the doctor."

Marvin dressed. "I want you to stay in bed. I'll have Candy bring you up some dry toast after we've eaten. That might stay down for you."

As he left, Betsy lay back, staring at the ceiling, thinking about how very much their lives would change with an infant in the house. She hoped she wasn't pregnant yet at the same time she hoped she was.

She could see herself sitting quietly, rocking a baby as she nursed him or her to sleep. The idea grew in her mind until she thought she would be very upset if she was wrong, and a baby wasn't on the way.

She had two healthy children, though, and though they weren't born of her body, the love she held for them was very real.

Candy knocked on the door and came in with a plate with two slices of plain toast on it. She sat down carefully on the edge of the bed, trying not to disturb Betsy too much. "Pa said you wanted this."

"I don't know about wanting it, but I'm hoping it will settle my stomach," Betsy said quietly.

"Pa already left to get the doctor." Candy watched her stepmother take a bite of the toast. "Pa said you had something to tell me."

Betsy smiled. "He's decided you can go to the church social with Steven after all. You'll need to ask him in the future because I won't be stuck in the middle again, but this time, you can go."

Candy squealed happily. "Oh, thank you, Betsy. I don't know how you did it, but I'm so happy. Do you want me to just sew today, or should I work on my bookwork without you?"

"I'd rather we did the bookwork together," Betsy said. "If you'll work on your dress this morning, I will try to do bookwork with you after breakfast."

Candy stayed until Betsy had eaten her full, and then she took the plate back down to the kitchen. "If you need anything, shout for me, and I'll be right here."

Betsy smiled as the girl left, and she sank back down to lie flat, which seemed to be the only position her stomach could even consider tolerating.

She dozed until Marvin came back with the doctor. After the doctor shooed her husband from the room, he started asking questions. She could tell he thought the same thing she did.

"I'm going to have to examine you," he said.

Betsy nodded. She'd expected that.

Ten minutes later, he said, "I would say you're definitely expecting. Looks like about two and a half months. Does that sound right to you?"

"Yes, it does."

The doctor smiled. "I'll send the midwife who works with me out to see you. Do you have any questions for me?"

She shook her head, immediately feeling ill again. "Would you send my husband back in, so I can tell him?"

"Of course," he said, opening the door to her husband in the hall.

"Is she all right, Doc?"

"You're going to have to ask your wife that question. I'll be on my way." The doctor walked around Marvin and down the stairs.

Marvin went into the bedroom and shut the door. He'd gotten very bad news from the same doctor about his first wife. "What did he say?" Marvin asked. "What's wrong?"

"I'm going to have a baby." Betsy smiled at him, hoping he'd be as pleased as she was.

"A baby. I... I don't know why I didn't think of that. It's no wonder you've been so sick."

"None at all," Betsy said.

"It never once occurred to me we could have more children. I brought you here to help me with the children I have, and not have more."

She bit her lip. "Are you upset?"

"Upset? Of course not. Just feeling a bit dense at the moment. Just think, we could have a girl as sweet as our Candy. Or a boy... Well, hopefully, a boy that wouldn't be quite as set on what he wants as our Tommy."

"I don't think I could handle getting notes from the teacher about Tommy and another child. Maybe we should rethink this whole thing..."

He chuckled. "It's much too late for that." He leaned down and kissed her forehead. "I need to get to work, but I'll tell Candy to take care of you."

"Do you mind if I tell her?" Betsy asked.

"Of course not. We'll tell Tommy at supper."

After he was gone, she lay there, imagining her waist growing as she carried a child. Oh, she couldn't wait to tell the children.

Candy came up a short while later to check on her, and Betsy patted the bed beside her. "We know what's wrong with me," Betsy said.

"We do? Is it terrible?" Candy burst into tears. "You're not dying, are you?"

Betsy smiled. "No, I'm not dying. I'm going to have a baby."

"So you and Pa are doing that thing you told me about!" Candy frowned at Betsy. "You can answer all my questions about it when I'm ready to marry."

"I will do my best," Betsy said. She really didn't want to talk about the intimate details of her marriage with Candy.

Candy wiped away her tears and stood up. "I'm going to have a baby sister or brother! You'd better start knitting red booties, just in case."

Betsy laughed softly. "That's probably a good idea."

AFTER SPENDING MOST of the day in bed, Betsy was able to eat supper with her family, carefully eating small bites, hoping it wouldn't trigger another bout of illness. Tommy stared at her raptly. "You're still sick?"

Marvin answered for her. "She's going to be sick for a while. She's having a baby."

Tommy looked at Betsy. "You have a baby in you now?" he asked.

"I do," Betsy responded.

"How'd it get in there?"

Candy immediately started giggling, and Tommy looked between his family members waiting for someone to explain. "We'll talk about it later," Marvin said. "Like in a year or two."

"But I want to know now!"

Betsy smiled. "So if it's a girl, what should we name her?"

Thankfully her question distracted the children from baby making, and they were able to finish the meal talking about potential names. "I think we should have another boy," Tommy said. "We'll name him Timothy, so we can have a Tommy and a Timmy."

"Or, we could have a girl named Amanda, and we can have a Candy and a Mandy."

Betsy grinned at Marvin. "I'll just be happy if it's healthy."

When they went to bed that night, Betsy snuggled into Marvin's side. "You feeling all right?" he asked.

"Much better than earlier. I seem to be having all day sickness instead of morning sickness."

"I've noticed. Kristen has some ideas. Tommy talked to her after supper."

"I'm so glad you're excited about the baby."

"Oh, trust me, I am." He kissed her nose. "Why wouldn't I want a baby with the woman I love? I mean, we already share Candy and

Tommy, but a child that came from both of us...it's the most natural thing in the world."

"Did you just say you love me?" she asked.

"Of course, I love you. You're the magnificent bride I've been needing for a very long time."

She laughed. "I love you too, but I'm just plain boring Betsy. Ask anyone."

"I'd never believe them even if they said it. You are exactly what I needed in a wife and then some." He kissed her softly. "Go to sleep, Betsy. You're sleeping for two now..."

Epilogue

Candy went back to school after the Christmas holidays, walking with her brother who was covered almost entirely in red. She'd made the decision to go back on her own, mostly because she wanted to spend more time with Steven, and her pa didn't let her see him often enough to suit her.

One night, in the middle of June, Betsy's pains started, and Marvin went for the midwife. Candy stayed with Betsy, holding her hand until the midwife arrived.

To Betsy's surprise, the midwife acted as if Candy had been her assistant for years, and she told her what to do, and even let her catch the baby.

After the midwife cut the umbilical cord, Candy stood holding the baby with tears streaming down her face. "Oh, Ma. She's beautiful!"

Already emotional from the birth of the baby, Betsy burst into tears. "You've never called me Ma!"

Candy smiled. "It's time. It'll be better if we all call you Ma. Less confusing for the baby."

The midwife took the baby to the bathroom and washed her up, bringing her back and putting her in her mother's arms. Candy stared at her for a bit, but finally said, "I should go tell Pa he has another daughter."

The midwife had finished cleaning Betsy up and said she'd be back in a few days to make sure Betsy and the baby were doing well.

As soon as she left, Marvin walked into the room, staring at the baby in Betsy's arms. "We never did settle on a name for her."

"No, we didn't. Let's name her Josie."

"I like that. Josephine, and we'll call her Josie?"

Betsy nodded. "She's so beautiful."

"She is. Are you all right?"

"Yes, I am. I have three beautiful children now."

"We probably need another dozen," Marvin said.

Betsy's eyes widened. "Let me recover from this one before we start talking about the next."

"I can do that. I love you, Betsy Small."

"And I love you."

IF YOU ENJOYED THIS book, make sure you go back and read all the books in the Brides of Beckham series.

To get notice of new books by Kirsten Osbourne, click here[1].

---

1. http://www.kirstenandmorganna.com/newsletter

Don't miss out!

Visit the website below and you can sign up to receive emails whenever Kirsten Osbourne publishes a new book. There's no charge and no obligation.

https://books2read.com/r/B-A-VSFD-KALGC

BOOKS 2 READ

Connecting independent readers to independent writers.

www.ingramcontent.com/pod-product-compliance
Lightning Source LLC
LaVergne TN
LVHW092336171025
823772LV00034B/313